'Goodnig

Russs's words cu... ...r that she was stil... ...naïve could you ...e, for heaven's sake! S... ...eing far too intense about it. She gave him a forced smile as she recovered her composure.

'Goodnight, Russ.'

She walked out into the hall, trying to play the role of hostess and appear as if nothing had happened. Well, it hadn't, had it?

Dear Reader

We have pleasure in introducing new author Rebecca Lang with MIDNIGHT SUN, set in Arctic Canada. Margaret Barker is back with THE DOCTOR'S DAUGHTER, then Judith Ansell and Marion Lennox take us to Australia, with HEARTS OUT OF TIME and ONE CARING HEART, both tear-jerkers! Enjoy your holiday reading.

The Editor

!!!STOP PRESS!!! If you enjoy reading these medical books, have you ever thought of writing one? We are always looking for new writers for LOVE ON CALL, and want to hear from you. Send for the guidelines, and start writing!

Margaret Barker pursued a variety of interesting careers before she became a full-time author. Besides holding a BA degree in French and linguistics, she is a Licentiate of the Royal Academy of Music, a state registered nurse and a qualified teacher. Happily married, she has two sons, a daughter, and an increasing number of grandchildren. She lives with her husband in a sixteenth-century thatched house near the sea.

Recent titles by the same author:

SURGEON'S DILEMMA
RED SEA REUNION

THE DOCTOR'S DAUGHTER

BY
MARGARET BARKER

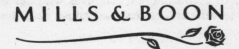

MILLS & BOON LIMITED
ETON HOUSE, 18-24 PARADISE ROAD
RICHMOND, SURREY TW9 1SR

MILLS & BOON, the Rose Device and LOVE ON CALL
are trademarks of the publisher.

First published in Great Britain 1994
by Mills & Boon Limited

© Margaret Barker 1994

Australian copyright 1994   Philippine copyright 1994
This edition 1994

ISBN 0 263 78706 0

Set in Times 10 on 11½ pt.

03-9407-44415

Made and printed in Great Britain

CHAPTER ONE

'WELL, he looks OK to me,' Lauren said, as she turned from the screen to look at her patient. 'Excellent heart-beat, obvious little masculine appendage; what more could you wish for?'

Jane Gregson giggled with relief. 'He didn't seem as active this weekend, Doctor. Usually he kicks me to bits.'

'Well, perhaps he was feeling a bit sluggish and didn't feel like exerting himself. Got a mind of his own already, your little boy, even if he won't give us a piece of it for another couple of months.'

'To be honest, Doctor, I wanted to have another scan just to check out that he really is a boy. Dave's set his heart on a boy and. . .'

'Well, you can reassure him on that,' Lauren said, a trifle briskly. She had a waiting-room full of patients and she was running late. A delivery up at Home Farm during the night had set her timetable back. She operated an appointments system but it soon fell down if either she or her medical partner Ian Fairburn were delayed. To be honest, she'd had no doubt in her mind that Jane Gregson's pregnancy was going along smoothly, but she always liked to reassure her mothers. Pamper your young mothers, her father had always told her, and they'll be nice and relaxed when they reach full term.

She helped Jane swing her legs over the side of the examination couch.

'How's your father getting along?' the young mother-to-be asked, as she slipped her feet back into comfy moccasins. Dr James Mansfield had brought her into the world twenty-three years ago and looked after her all through her childhood, in fact until just three months ago when he'd suffered a stroke. He was a great favourite with all his patients, who were glad that his daughter was carrying on the family practice.

The worried expression on Lauren's face deepened. All the patients asked after her father, and while it was very touching, it took up so much time. She was constantly battling against the clock, trying to do two things at once, running the surgery as well as keeping an eye on the day-to-day household tasks. Her father's sister, Aunt Maud, did her best, but she wasn't getting any younger and Lauren had to help out whenever she could.

She scraped a hand through her unruly ginger hair, her fingers catching in the crimpy curls that built up if she didn't brush through it every few hours. The burning bush, some of her friends had called this constant source of irritation when she was at school. That was the more polite description! Others had nick-named her Birdie because of her impossible nest.

'Dad's doing fine.' Lauren reached for Jane Gregson's large woollen cardigan and helped her into it. 'He's getting bored now, so he must be improving. But he gets so frustrated with himself. He can't use his right hand and his speech is still slow.'

'Give him my love,' Jane said, easing herself towards the door that Lauren had now opened.

Lauren smiled. 'I will.' She looked out into the waiting-room. The cushioned seats were grouped around a central island of magazines and there was a toy corner over by the front window, where a couple of little boys were making varied animal noises as they built a Duplo zoo.

'Sorry I'm running late, everybody.' Lauren's eyes scanned the sea of faces. 'Had an unexpected delivery last night and——'

'Was it Samantha?' asked a young woman in a dark blue anorak and jeans.

'Yes, it was.' Lauren tried to escape back into her room.

'What did she have. . .not another boy, was it?'

'It was, as a matter of fact.'

'Three boys, she's got. Still, Peter'll get plenty of help on the farm when that lot grow up. I know Sam was wanting a girl but I expect. . .'

Lauren smiled as she closed the door. The nice thing about working in a family practice was that everybody knew everybody else. The older patients still treated her like a child, hardly believing that at thirty she was capable of doing the work her father and her grandfather had always done.

Quickly, she tapped the details of Jane Gregson's visit into her computer. She'd had a great deal of opposition from her father when she'd tried to update the surgery, but the system was now working well. She still had to set up a computer in her father's consulting-room and she made a mental note to get it done before the new locum arrived next week. She intended to move upstairs to the holy of holies and let the new man take over her room.

Lauren leaned across to the intercom and spoke to the practice nurse at Reception.

'Who's next, Ruth?' She waited, ready to call up the patient's details on her computer.

'Our new locum has just arrived, this very moment, but he's insisting on seeing you. I told him you were busy but. . .'

'He'll have to wait till the end of surgery, Ruth. Actually, I was just thinking about him and planning to. . .'

Lauren stopped in mid-sentence as the door opened. A tall man with fair, sandy hair walked in, closed the door behind him and advanced towards her, his hand outstretched.

She frowned, ignoring the hand. Over the intercom she could hear Ruth apologising. 'You could hand him over to Dr Fairburn, Dr Lauren. Would you like. . .?'

'It's OK, Ruth. Give me two minutes before you brief me on the next patient.'

Lauren leaned back in her chair. 'We weren't expecting you until next week, Dr— er——' She searched her brain for the name on the locum's file that the health authority had sent her.

'Call me Russ.' The new doctor gave her a confident smile and sank down into the armchair at the side of Lauren's desk.

Lauren had specially designed her room so that there was a long desk against the window on which she kept her computer and paperwork. A couple of armchairs pulled against the desk meant that she was able to see eyeball to eyeball with her patients and there was no barrier between them. At this precise moment she wished she'd stuck to the old arrangement of doctor sitting behind desk. This new locum was too cocky by half. And by the look of that suntan he appeared as if he'd just got back from some exotic holiday. . .ah, now she remembered. His CV said that he'd been working in West Africa. That might account for the casual nature of his clothes. Cream linen trousers, open-necked shirt beneath a flamboyant check patterned stone coloured jacket.

Dr Russell Harvey kept the smile glued to his face as he studied the irate looking woman beside him. He'd been warned by the medical employment agency that she could be a tartar but he hadn't expected such a cold reception. What had they called her? Miss Prim! How very apt! She looked as if her face would crack if she smiled. Couldn't be much more than thirty-five but behaved like a woman of fifty. The last time he'd seen thick brogue shoes like those they'd been on the feet of the old matron at his boarding school and she'd been at least a hundred—or so he'd thought at the time.

'I'm afraid I can't show you round or explain the job until the end of the morning. As you can see, I've got a lot of patients waiting to see me. If you'd telephoned to let me know you were coming. . .'

'Look, don't worry.' Russ leaned across and placed a hand on Lauren's arm.

He felt her flinch at the contact and withdrew his hand quickly. This one really was an ice maiden. He'd have to tread carefully.

'Don't worry,' he repeated, in what was meant to be a conciliatory tone. 'I got here a week early so I've got a week to spare. Give me a consulting-room and I'll halve the patients with you.'

'Oh, I don't think I could do that. You see, they choose who they want to see. There's Dr Fairburn along the corridor and I'm in here and. . .'

'I can see that.' He smiled, enjoying the touch of femininity that was creeping into Lauren Mansfield's tone as she blustered. 'So, let me go out and see who's in a hurry and would like me to deal with them.'

He was on his feet, walking towards the door, opening it. Lauren stood rooted to the spot.

This new doctor was taking over her domain, threatening her territory.

'Look, I don't think——' she began, but he wasn't listening.

'Hello, everybody. I'm Dr Russell Harvey,' the newcomer was telling the patients in the waiting-room. 'Dr Mansfield is rushed off her feet this morning, so if any of you would like to see me I'm available in. . .' He turned to look at Lauren. 'Which room shall I work in, Doctor?'

All eyes were on Lauren. She swallowed hard. 'The upstairs consulting-room is free,' she announced through clenched teeth. 'That's my father's consulting-room. I'll show you the way.'

She ran up the stairs and pushed open the door.

Russell Harvey followed, admiring the lithe way the doctor moved. I bet she was good at athletics before she chose to become a staid country doctor, he was thinking, as he went into the consulting-room.

'Let's open the window,' he said, disliking the closed-in atmosphere. He walked across the room and flung open the casement. Looking out across the water meadows towards the swirling brown river, he remembered one of the reasons why he'd decided to take this post: to get out and about and enjoy the English countryside. He'd been too long exiled in the Third World.

'Make yourself at home,' Lauren said, with barely concealed sarcasm.

Russ turned around from the window. 'Oh, I always do. I travel a lot so I have to get to grips with my new surroundings as soon as I arrive.'

'So I see,' Lauren said. Something about the way the mild April breeze was ruffling this man's hair awakened a flicker of interest. He was a handsome brute—and didn't he know it! 'You won't find much technological equipment in here. My father is firmly rooted in the past, but I'm going to make some changes. There's the intercom which can be used, but that's about it. The receptionist will have to send the patients up complete with a printout of their notes.'

'I don't mind how they arrive here or what they bring with them. I'm not desperately fond of case histories, either on paper or computer. I prefer talking to the patient.'

'We insist on keeping our records up to date, Dr Harvey.' Lauren's tone was severe, specifically designed to show the man who was boss and put him in his place. 'I hope you will remember that.'

Russ strode across the room and sat down behind the desk, smoothing out a wrinkle on the old blotter. 'Yes, ma'am,' he replied, breezily. 'Now, perhaps you would be good enough to let me get on with some work. Send the first patient up, there's a good girl.'

Lauren turned and fumed her way down the stairs. I don't believe this is happening to me! she thought. This man, taking over my father's room. She must put her plans into action and move her own things up there, to emphasise that she was senior partner. The trouble was that she wouldn't have time until the weekend to organise the new computer, and now she'd actually got Dr Russell Harvey in there. Well, she'd soon get him out!

She went across to see Ruth at the reception counter.
Good, solid, dependable Ruth would know how to
handle the situation. In her mid-forties, Lauren's practice nurse managed her own home, husband, three
children and a full-time job at the surgery. Yet Lauren
had never seen her flustered or bad-tempered.

'If any patients offer to go up to see Dr Harvey
and. . .what's the matter, Ruth?'

The nurse was smiling broadly. 'There's no lack of
volunteers, Dr Lauren. Especially among the younger
women,' she whispered.

'Good. Well, take the first patient up, then,' Lauren
said, annoyed at the pique she felt. She couldn't help
admitting to herself that she'd hoped to leave the inter-
loper high and dry in his ivory tower.

Still, it was kind of him to offer to help, said a gentle
voice inside her head. It was the tiny voice that always
spoke to her when she was at her fiercest. She tried
so hard to be strong, to be as strong as a man would
be in her profession. . .to be the son her father had
hoped for but never had. And sometimes she overdid
the fierceness. She knew she did, but she didn't know
what to do about it. She couldn't give in and become
a soft fluffy creature like her sisters. They didn't have
all the responsibilities she had.

The door opened and Lauren concentrated all her
attention on Gwendoline Barrat and her one-year-old
daughter, Tracy.

'So you saw Mr Jones at Great Ormond Street last
week, didn't you, Gwendoline? I've had a letter from
him about Tracy and. . .'

'Oh, he was ever so nice, Dr Lauren. I feel so
relieved it's nothing serious.'

Lauren's fingers were gently palpating the large

strawberry mark on the side of young Tracy's temple. She'd had no doubt that the birth mark was a benign naevus, a localised patch of thickened and dilated blood vessels, which would disappear in the early years of Tracy's childhood. But the young mother had needed reassurance and it was always comforting to be told by a specialist the same words that your own doctor had said.

'They told me at Great Ormond Street that it'll disappear by the time Tracy's four,' Gwendoline Barrat recounted happily. 'I get so tired of telling people there's nothing wrong with her. Then they ask me if I had a forceps delivery, which I didn't, did I?'

Lauren shook her head. 'Just tell everybody what the specialist said and that will keep them quiet. They all mean well but it can get a bit wearying for you, especially when you've been so worried.'

'I'm not worried now, Dr Lauren.'

'Glad to hear it.'

Lauren chatted on with her patient, wanting to make sure that there was nothing else on her mind. The minute hand on the large clock above the door was moving relentlessly.

She showed Gwendoline out and spoke to Ruth over the intercom as she tapped in the details on her computer.

The door burst open and Lauren's medical partner Dr Ian Fairburn filled the doorway with his large, rugby-forward frame encased in an impeccable grey suit, not a dark hair on his head out of place.

'Who's up in your father's room?'

Lauren turned from the computer screen. Ian sounded more than a bit put out. He was usually such an affable person. She wondered what could have upset him.

'It's the new locum, Russell Harvey.'

Ian frowned. 'I thought he wasn't due till next week. Why did you set him on to work? We don't know anything at all about the man.'

Lauren bridled. 'We know a great deal about him—on paper, that is. You don't think I'd have let him start work without checking him out? He's been working for the World Health Organisation in Africa. They've given him six months' home leave and he's chosen to work here for three months. Hasn't worked in England for a few years, apparently.'

'Well, that'll be a great help! So long as the patients have beri beri or malaria we're sure to get accurate diagnoses.'

Lauren stood up. At five feet ten inches she had always found her height to be an advantage in difficult professional situations. Ian Fairburn was still taller than she was but not much. 'Look, he's a qualified doctor, with good references. We need another pair of hands. . .'

'And a brain.'

'A brain would be useful, I agree. Talking of which, perhaps you could put yours to good use, Ian. . .yes, what is it?' she barked, irritably, at the buzzing intercom.

'I'd like you to come up here right away.'

Lauren swallowed hard as she recognised Russell Harvey's voice. 'Why? Is there something you can't handle?'

'I want a second opinion. I've no doubt about the diagnosis myself, but I thought you, as senior partner, should confirm my suspicions.'

Lauren was immediately alerted by the serious tone of the new doctor's voice. 'What's your provisional diagnosis, Dr Harvey?'

'Meningitis.'

Lauren drew in her breath. 'I'll be right with you.'

CHAPTER TWO

LAUREN took the stairs two at a time. The door to her father's consulting-room was wide open. On the examination couch lay a small, motionless boy, his mother and father hovering anxiously beside him as Russell Harvey checked on the telltale symptoms.

'Dr Lauren, Ruth sent us straight up as soon as we arrived. Is Michael going to be all right?' the mother blurted out, tearfully.

'We'll do what we can, Mrs Smithson,' Lauren replied, with a calmness she didn't feel.

She remembered the Smithson family, who lived not far away from the surgery. Mr Smithson was a teacher at the local primary school and his wife was a full-time housewife.

Their only son Michael must be about three now, she thought, glancing at the notes on the desk to confirm. She hadn't seen him for some time, not since he was a baby, actually. In fact he was one of a small list of children who hadn't turned up for all their vaccinations. She'd already drafted out a letter to the parents, due to go out as soon as Ruth could arrange it.

Lauren felt a tingle of apprehension about the situation. She'd made a point of telling all her patients to bring in their children for the new vaccination against meningitis. It had only been available for a short time. Some of the parents had failed to respond and she was now in the process of chasing them up.

As she looked at the worried faces of Brian and

Mary Smithson she knew that this was not the time to bring up the question of vaccination.

She put her hand on Michael's forehead, feeling the burning skin.

Russell Harvey held the thermometer in front of her so she could check the reading. A hundred and two point five. She felt the back of Michael's head at the place where it joined with the neck. It was rigid, retracted and stiff. But it was the characteristic purpuric rash on the skin which was the single most convincing symptom in the diagnosis.

'I'm going to do a lumbar puncture,' Russell Harvey told Lauren in a quiet, urgent voice.

Lauren nodded. 'There's a sterile pack in that cupboard.' She turned to look at Michael's parents. 'We're going to take some fluid from Michael's spine to decide what treatment to give him. Would you like to stay up here or go back to the waiting-room for a few minutes?'

'Mummy! Don't go!' Michael whimpered, reaching out his small hand.

'I won't leave you, Michael,' Mary Smithson said, squeezing her little boy's hand. She looked up at Lauren. 'I'll stay here, Doctor, but my husband doesn't like injections or needles.'

Lauren glanced at Mr Smithson and saw that he was very pale. 'Injections can be very necessary sometimes,' she said, quietly. 'If. . .' She had been about to mention the life-saving properties of vaccinations but decided to hold her tongue. The poor father was suffering enough as it was, so she changed what she was going to say.

'If you'd like to go downstairs, I'm sure Ruth will be glad to give you a cup of tea while you wait.'

Lauren couldn't help but be impressed with the speed and efficiency of her new locum. He'd already scrubbed up and was preparing the skin on Michael's back. Swiftly, he inserted the lumbar puncture needle between the vertebrae. Young Michael didn't move and appeared not to have felt anything.

Lauren filled a sterile test tube with the cerebro-spinal fluid that gushed out. It was obviously under pressure, another sign of meningitis, and the turgid appearance led her to believe that on testing the fluid they would find an increased number of white blood cells.

'I think we'd better get Michael into hospital,' she told Mrs Smithson, gently. 'I'll ask Ruth to call up the ambulance.'

'I suppose you've got some sulphadiazine in your dispensary?' Russell Harvey asked. 'I think we should start anti-bacterial treatment immediately rather than wait for the laboratory diagnosis.'

Lauren nodded in agreement as she instructed Ruth over the intercom to order the ambulance and bring up the necessary medication.

'It's serious, isn't it, Dr Lauren?' The mother's eyes were wet with tears.

Lauren drew in her breath. This was the bit she always found difficult. . .how to be truthful, and yet soften the blow.

'We're starting treatment immediately, so Michael has a good chance of. . .of getting over this. He's a strong boy and. . .'

'Has he got meningitis, Doctor?'

'I think he may have,' Lauren said, carefully. 'But we can't be certain until the laboratory tests have been made.'

The mother rubbed her hand over her eyes. 'I saw a programme on the telly about it, just a few weeks ago. And the little boy in the film had a stiff neck. . . just like Michael's. They were telling you to get your children injected against it with this new wonder vaccine, but Brian said he thought it might be dangerous.'

Russell Harvey was looking intently at the mother. Lauren didn't trust herself to speak.

'So you decided to leave it to chance,' Russell said, quietly.

'I. . .I didn't actually decide to do anything,' Mary Smithson said. 'Brian makes all the decisions in our house.'

Lauren looked across at Russell Harvey and saw her own anxiety mirrored in his deep blue eyes. Her locum was more sensitive than she'd given him credit for when he first arrived.

She went back to her room after Michael and his parents had gone off in the ambulance. The needless emergency had left her feeling drained. She put it down to lack of sleep, but it was also the frustration of meeting a situation that need never have arisen. She thought about the young mother who was content to let her husband make all the decisions. Had there been no progress since the days when women were subservient to their men? Couldn't Mary Smithson think for herself?

As she waited for Ruth to send up the next patient, she found herself feeling glad that she would never have to face the situation of living with a man who had his own pigheaded ideas and imposed them on everybody else. In a way, it was that which gave her life a sense of purpose: to know that she was her own boss and always would be.

She realised that her decision never to marry had been a conscious one after a particularly unpleasant experience during her early years as a medical student. Before then, she'd intended to have both a career and marriage, when she met the right man. She'd known it wouldn't be easy combining the two, but she'd been in no doubt she could have handled it. But since that awful day when. . .

She took in a deep breath and deliberately blanked out the twelve-year-old memories. She wasn't one to dwell on the past, being more interested in what was going on at the moment. Her life was very full and very rewarding and, as far as marriage was concerned, Aunt Maud had told her often when she was young that she wouldn't miss much by staying single.

'Who wants to be a man's skivvy, when you've got brains and a good profession! And think how fortunate you are to be able to carry on the family tradition, behaving like the elder son your father always wanted.'

Aunt Maud's philosophy had been drilled into her from an early age. Her father's sister had been a very successful and well respected headmistress who had taken early retirement twelve years before to supervise her brother's household when Lauren's mother had died. Since then she'd ruled the roost in the Mansfield family and Lauren had always looked up to her. Even now, in fact especially now, when Aunt Maud was nearing seventy, Lauren found it hard to contradict her.

By twelve o'clock all the patients had been seen. Ian had gone out to do the house calls, so Lauren was at last free to meet her new locum in a more relaxed manner. Well, as relaxed as she could get under the circumstances. She intended to keep her distance and make sure that Russell Harvey toed the line. Three months could be a long time if she allowed him to walk all over her. He seemed a very strong character—which was good in a professional situation requiring bold decisions—but could be difficult to handle over matters of practice policy. Her father had been a stickler for discipline among his staff and Lauren intended to keep up his exacting standards to the letter.

She tried to contact Russell Harvey on the intercom. He didn't answer. She tapped her fingers impatiently on the desk for half a minute before buzzing Ruth.

'I'm trying to locate Dr Harvey. Do you. . .?'

'He's here with me, Dr Lauren. We're going through some records together. Would you like to speak to him?'

Lauren heard the breathless quality in Ruth's voice. Old married woman she may be, but she could still be flattered by the attentions of a handsome doctor!

'No, I'll come through.'

Russell Harvey was sitting in front of the spare computer screen, the one destined for her father's surgery, or rather the surgery she planned to take over.

'I'll fix this up in my room this afternoon.' The new doctor turned and smiled at her.

'Actually, that's going to be my room. I'd planned to move up there before you arrived.'

'What's wrong with the room you've got?'

'If you don't mind, I happen to be senior partner here, so I'll decide who works from which room.'

'But of course!' The smile broadened. 'I wouldn't dream of upsetting you.' Dear God! The poor girl was desperate in her power struggle. She couldn't let up for an instant. She was as rigid as a block of steel.

Ruth was hurriedly gathering up her handbag and slipping into her outdoor coat.

'I'll come back after lunch for the well-woman clinic, Dr Lauren,' she said, beating a hasty retreat through the front door. She'd seen her boss giving lectures to medical staff who'd quaked in their shoes, but this man looked as if he was actually enjoying the situation.

The front door closed behind Ruth. Russell Harvey did a complete turn on the office chair before leaping off and leaning over the reception counter.

'Alone at last!' he said, his smile turning into a broad grin that was designed to infuriate Lauren. 'What do we do for lunch here?'

'We don't do anything,' Lauren replied stiffly. Really, the man was being impossibly familiar with her! 'We all go our separate ways. I'll fill you in on the workings of the surgery before you go, so that you'll know what's happening when you start work next week. Incidentally, thanks for your help this morning,' she added, quietly. 'I'll give you a form to fill in so you can claim your fee.'

'I don't need a form to claim my fee. I've already decided to take you out to lunch. That's the price you have to pay for my invaluable services this morning.'

'I've told you I don't eat lunch.'

'That's why you're so scraggy. A tall girl like you should have more flesh on her bones. There's a restaurant just a few miles from Ongar that I want to try. I read about it in the *Good Food Guide*. Come on, where's your coat?'

Lauren opened her mouth to speak but for once she was lost for words.

'Dr Harvey. . .'

'Look, I've asked you to call me Russ. I'm going to

call you Lauren whether you like it or not. We'll be
working together for the next three months so we might
as well get to know each other. Come on, we'll take
my car.'

'I'll get my coat,' she muttered, moving to the staff
cloakroom at the back of Reception. There was an
unreality about the situation that seemed to be knocking the stuffing out of her. She decided it must be the
lack of sleep that was making her so docile.

She stood in front of the mirror as she shrugged her
arms into her large camel coat. It could do with a
clean, but whenever she'd thought about it she'd wondered what she would wear in the meantime. It was
getting a bit shabby too. . .positively threadbare on
the elbows. She could invest in a new one, but Aunt
Maud would think it a wicked waste of money when
the coat was only. . .how old was it? Heavens! It must
be four years old at least. Perhaps she'd treat herself
to a day in London when she could get a whole day off.

Russell Harvey was standing by the front door when
she emerged. She saw the critical look as his eyes
scanned her appearance. Oh, God! She was sure he
must be comparing her with the other women he took
out to lunch. A man like that would be used to taking
out sophisticated, well groomed women. She couldn't
think, for the life of her, why he wanted her to go
with him for lunch. They could have concluded their
business here in a few minutes and gone their
separate ways.

She went out into the car park. 'You can let the
door slam shut, Dr Harvey. It's on a Yale lock and
we've all got our own keys.'

She stopped in her tracks as she saw the sleek and
shiny car standing beside her own mud-spattered Ford

Fiesta. Dr Harvey's car was a brand new black BMW. Lauren knew very little about cars but she could see at a glance that this one would be very powerful on the road. She hoped her new locum wasn't going to raise hell on the narrow country lanes.

He must have sensed her anxiety because he drove at a reasonable speed along the twisty twiny roads that pierced the gently undulating countryside between the Oakwood village surgery and Ongar. A squally April shower had blown up and the rhythmic thud thud of the windscreen wipers began to lull Lauren off to sleep. She realised that she couldn't have had more than three hours' sleep the night before. She'd been called out at midnight, just as she was turning in, and she'd delivered the new baby at Home Farm at half-past two.

It occurred to her that they would soon be passing near to Home Farm. Ian Fairburn had a long list of house calls to make and maybe he wouldn't get to Home Farm until quite late. Perhaps she should call in now and see if all was well.

'Slow down, Russ.' She felt a pang of annoyance that she'd at last complied with the wretched man's insistence she call him by that idiotic abbreviation of a perfectly good name. Oh, well, it hadn't hurt her, had it? 'I'd like to take a couple of minutes to call in on my new mother and the baby born last night, or rather this morning.'

Russ eased his foot off the accelerator. 'So that's why you're looking like death warmed up. Or do you always take morning surgery with no make-up on and hair that looks as if it's never seen a hairbrush?'

'I expect you always shower your lunch guests with such extravagant compliments, don't you?' Lauren retorted, but allowed her hand to furtively steal inside her handbag. She had a lipstick somewhere. . .but would it do any good? And anyway, how dared the man make personal remarks about her appearance? As if she cared! Well, maybe she'd just nip into the cloakroom when they got to this restaurant place. She'd heard it was very posh and terribly expensive so she ought to smarten up a bit. She would make the effort to drag a comb through her hair.

'Stop here!'

'Yes, ma'am!'

The tyres screeched on the wet road surface. Lauren looked down the little road that led to Home Farm. Ian Fairburn's car was parked outside.

'No point in duplicating a visit,' Lauren said. 'I'll let Ian deal with it.'

Russ let in the clutch and the car moved forward.

'I had the distinct impression that Dr Fairburn took a dislike to me this morning.'

'I think that's an understatement. He didn't like the way you marched in and took over. Neither did I, to be honest. Exactly why did you turn up a week early?'

'That's what I like about you, Laurie. . .the intense gratitude shown for services rendered.'

'My name is Lauren, not Laurie. I'm stretching a point by allowing you to call me by my first name after such a short acquaintance. . .'

'Oh, spare me the scene from Jane Austen! "Such a short acquaintance"!' he mimicked. 'Now, can we return to the twentieth century, *Lauren*?' He emphasised her name. 'You wanted to know why I arrived early. It's quite simple. I finished my work in Africa sooner than expected, so I got an earlier flight and decided to come straight to the wilds of Essex, and book into a hotel while I search for an apartment.'

She was bristling from his rudeness in taking the mickey out of her. But at the same time she was curious about the man. . .and as senior partner she ought to find out all she could about him. She remembered reading in his CV that he'd been a senior registrar at Guy's Hospital before joining the World Health Organisation. She couldn't remember any details about marital status so she ought to get that out of the way.

'So you haven't any family ties, I take it.'

He took his eyes off the road for a split-second to give her a withering glance. 'Would I be free to spend years at a time in the Third World countries if I did? Of course, now I remember it, I left my wife and ten children in a mangrove swamp because they were costing too much to feed.'

She ignored his bantering tone and swallowed her pride. 'I simply ask because there's a bachelor flat over the garage at the surgery. I could let you have it for a nominal rent.' Aunt Maud had been on at her for months to let out the flat and there would be the added bonus of a qualified doctor on the premises.

'What about Ian Fairburn? Where does he live?'

'With his parents in the village. We went to school together. Well, he was a couple of years older than me.'

'How cosy. The boy next door working in the family firm. I bet you get on like a house on fire. No wonder he doesn't want me muscling in on his cosy set-up.'

'Don't be silly! Ian and I are just good friends.'

Russ's loud guffaw took Lauren totally by surprise. It was true that, just occasionally, she'd had a twinge of doubt about Ian's proprietorial attitude towards her, wondering what his motives were, but she always dismissed the idea as being fanciful.

'I wasn't suggesting there was anything between you,' Russ declared, in an amused tone. 'I can see you've decided to remain the eternal virgin. "Chaste, never chased" is your motto, I would imagine, isn't it?'

'Whatever gave you that idea?' Lauren was incensed by his rudeness.

Again, Russ took his eyes from the wheel. 'Well, I mean, look at you! Thick, serviceable shoes. . .'

'I'm a doctor. I have to tramp through muddy farmyards!'

'Plenty of women do that but they manage to keep their femininity. Buy yourself some green wellies to slip on and off in the car. Put some make-up on. . . not a lot, just enough to show you're not planning on staying single for the rest of your life.'

'But I am!'

'Oh, well, that accounts for it.'

'I don't need a man in my life. I like my work. I have a pleasant home life. My father, Aunt Maud, my sisters. . .'

She broke off, furious with herself for being on the defensive. She didn't have to account to this man for anything. He was overstepping the mark by interrogating her like this.

'Tell me about Aunt Maud. She sounds fascinating!'

'I owe a great deal to my father's sister. When my mother died, she took early retirement from her job as a headmistress so that she could run the household. I was just starting out at medical school; my two sisters—they're twins—were only sixteen and something of a handful. But Aunt Maud had got used to dealing with them when she'd visited us in the holidays and she kept them under control. She ran the house in the same way she'd run her school and everybody respected her. When she first moved in we didn't have a practice nurse so she used to write the letters, help out in the surgery, answer the phone. . .everything a doctor's wife had to do. Except she was only my father's sister, not his wife.'

'Why do you say only? I expect she thought she was every bit as good as being a doctor's wife.'

'Aunt Maud is proud to be single! Proud of having chosen her way of life.'

'So you thought you'd be just like her, did you?'

'I must admit, I admire her strength of character.'

'I expect you'll get your wish—about not getting married, I mean.'

'It's not a wish—it's a conscious decision.'

'To devote yourself to the general public, to a life of service. Very commendable.'

'You're making fun of me again. . .but I don't mind. It's water off a duck's back.'

He glanced sideways again. 'I wouldn't think you're easily upset, are you?'

She shook her head. 'It takes a lot to knock me off my perch.'

'So when did you decide to give up normal human feelings and failings and become Miss Prim?'

They were pulling up in front of an impressive Georgian mansion set back from the main road. Although it was the middle of the day, lights twinkled out from every window. The door to a wide, oak-beamed hall was open invitingly. It was so long since Lauren had been to a place like this. On the odd occasion when she sallied forth to a local concert with Ian Fairburn they staved off the pangs of hunger in the nearest snack bar.

'Miss Prim. . .is that what you think I am?'

She saw his eyes flicker as he switched off the engine and turned towards her. There was something about the expression in his eyes that disturbed her. She noticed again that they were deepest blue, over-shadowed by strong, sand-coloured eyebrows that merged with the strands of hair falling like wings on both sides of his forehead. His hair was far too long—for a respectable doctor, that was. If he'd been a pop star or a film director it would have been appropriate. She wouldn't have given him a second glance. But for a few seconds, she found her eyes riveted to his face.

'Isn't that how you would like everyone to think of you?'

'You're very impertinent.'

He laughed. 'And you're desperately out of date, Lauren. Impertinence isn't a word that's used outside nineteenth-century novels or girls' finishing schools.'

'I just happen to think good manners are important.'

'And there I would agree with you.'

Suddenly, he'd dropped the bantering tone.

'You would?' she said, almost in disbelief.

He ran round and opened the car door. 'Allow me.' He swept his arm out sideways in the semblance of a courteous gesture.

She stepped out, her arm brushing against his. The close contact caught her unawares. She enjoyed the flicker of excitement that ran down her arm and tingled into her fingers. Mmm. . .that might be a nice feeling if she let it grow on her. She didn't approve of this man, but she enjoyed talking to him. . .even if he did try to make fun of her all the time. He was a stimulating sparring partner. You would never get bored with a man like this. She stiffened as he put his hand under her arm but she decided it would be churlish to pull herself away. He was, after all, her escort for lunch at this very swanky establishment. And to think, she'd been contemplating grabbing a piece of cheese and an apple to eat at her desk!

As Russ put his hand under Lauren's arm and led her towards the door of the restaurant he was thinking that it would probably have been more fun to have brought Lauren's Aunt Maud out to lunch. But he regarded her as a challenge. He had to break through that outer veneer of cold indifference if he was going to work with the woman. He couldn't bear a stiff working relationship. The patients didn't like it either. He'd seen how tender and warm she could be with her patients. It was only when she spoke to him that she put up the barriers. What on earth had dammed up her feelings and emotions?

CHAPTER THREE

YE GODS! This comb was useless! Lauren stared at her
reflection. What a mess she felt, so totally out of place
even here in the ladies' powder room; especially here,
in fact, with its thick white carpet, china dishes of
dried rose-petals, gold-plated taps gleaming above the
impeccably spotless washbasins. She almost expected
a geisha girl to emerge from behind the chintz curtains
to run the water for her!

As she rubbed her wet hands on the scented soap
she decided that it was all a bit like Harrods without
the crowds. If only she'd gone straight into the restaurant with Russ instead of excusing herself the
minute she'd stepped inside the place! But as soon as
the receptionist had removed the comfort of her old
camel coat she'd felt as if she were naked. That coat
had covered a multitude of sins, like the frayed cuffs
on her white cotton shirt and the shiny sitting marks
on her grey woollen skirt. But she knew full well that
if she stayed in here titivating her appearance until
midnight it wouldn't make any difference.

Why bother anyway? she asked herself. Let Russell
Harvey insult her all he liked! He was only here for
three months, and if he became too intolerable she
would find some excuse to get rid of him.

He was leaning against a small bar that led off from
the entrance hall when she finally emerged, treading
her way cautiously through the mini-jungle of expensive potted plants. The temperature, she noticed, was

31

in keeping with the exotic tropical ambience, making her sense an unwelcome attack of nervous perspiration setting in.

'What will you have?'

'A bloody Mary.'

His eyes flickered but he refrained from making any comment as he passed on the unexpected order to the barman.

Lauren permitted herself an inward giggle. She had no idea what a bloody Mary was, let alone what it would taste like. She'd heard Bette Davis ordering the drink in an old black and white film and she was feeling reckless for once. Hopefully, her outrageous choice would spur her drinking partner on to make a rude remark.

'Ice, madam?' the barman asked.

Lauren eyed the large frozen rock, poised on the end of a curved stainless steel instrument that looked like a gynaecological speculum, reminding her briefly that she must on no account actually drink her probably intoxicating drink, because she was in charge of the well-woman clinic that afternoon. She would pretend to sip it and then tip it surreptitiously into a convenient plant pot, praying that she wouldn't poison anything.

She cleared her throat. 'Of course.'

As Russell Harvey tried to cover a smile with his hand, Lauren couldn't help noticing the thick sun-whitened hairs that ran from his wrist to his fingertips. If he'd been dark, he would have looked like a gorilla, she thought, inconsequentially, as she accepted her drink. Heavens! The glass was cold. . .and a good thing too. It would cool down her sweaty fingers.

'So what was so amusing?' she asked, as the barman moved away.

'I was thinking how worldly wise you seemed all of a sudden. How long have you been drinking bloody Marys?'

Out of bravado she took a tiny sip and almost choked. 'About five seconds.'

He laughed. 'That's what I thought.'

Lauren leaned against the bar for support and picked up one of the huge menus.

'It's like studying for a degree in gastronomy,' she remarked as she skimmed through the pages. 'A large part of the world is starving and we're here gorging ourselves.'

'We do all we can for the Third World,' he observed, quietly. 'But it doesn't harm anyone to have the occasional feast.'

'I'll have the monkfish and a green salad.'

'No starter?' the waiter queried.

She shook her head. 'I don't normally eat lunch.'

'What do you normally do at lunchtime?' Russ asked, handing back the menus to the waiter after ordering a pepper steak.

'I work straight through the day. My aunt takes care of my father so I don't have to go home. I like to get as much as I can done before the evening surgery.'

'Would you say you were a workaholic?'

'Never really thought about it. I suppose I might be. I just get on with the next job in hand.'

'But you should take time off, to reassess where you're going.'

She frowned. 'How do you mean?'

'Well, if you just keep chasing around like a dog after its tail, you may well be going round in circles. If you relaxed a bit more you'd have time to work out where you're going. For instance, what are your future ambitions, Lauren?'

'Oh, my God! You're beginning to sound like a television interviewer. Don't be so nosy. . .well, if you must know, I've achieved everything I set out to do. I qualified as a doctor, took over the family surgery, followed in my father's and my grandfather's footsteps and. . .well, what more do I want?'

'And what about sex?'

Lauren spluttered into her bloody Mary and flung the question back at him. 'What do you mean, what about sex?'

'Why do you try to create the impression that you're some kind of neutered animal?'

'You've got a nerve!'

'Yes, haven't I? It comes in useful at times. Our table's ready now, so let's go in.'

A neutered animal! What a horrible thing to say. Lauren was inwardly seething from the insult as she threaded her way towards the corner table where the waiter was holding back her chair.

She looked across the starched white tablecloth, straight through the lighted candelabrum at this ogre of a man, and surprised herself by feeling a rush of something akin to desire. His deliberatedly brutal words seemed to have kick-started a reluctant awareness of her own long-ignored sexuality. For a few seconds she found herself wondering what a sexual encounter with a man like Russell Harvey would be like. Her eyes were drawn to his full, sensuous lips, his strong determined jawline, the thick, sandy stubble already showing around his suntanned chin. He would have to shave twice a day if he weren't to rub her skin. Once again, she couldn't help remembering the roughness of Peter Hardcastle's jaw during that awful experience twelve years ago.

Without thinking, she put her hand to her mouth, running her fingers over the place where she'd felt sore.

'Are you feeling OK?'

She put on her bright professional smile. 'Of course. I was just remembering that I've got to be back by two-thirty. So I hope they don't take too long to serve us.'

'Relax. There's plenty of time. And I'd like to say that you should smile more often. You look much more. . .feminine.'

'You mean not so neutered.'

'Definitely not at all neutered.'

The atmosphere was getting better by the minute, Lauren decided. From then on, she made a point of keeping the conversation light and impersonal. The monkfish was delicious, the salad suitably crisp and she allowed herself to be persuaded into a crème caramel, the sort of pudding that Aunt Maud never got around to making. It was only when they were sipping their coffee that she decided to broach the subject uppermost in her mind.

'Tell me why you decided to take a job as a locum. I would have thought you'd have wanted to have a holiday after the rigours of working in the tropics.'

'I need the money.'

Lauren frowned in disbelief as she remembered the expensive car Russ had just parked. 'Come on, pull the other one! That fabulous car outside. . .'

'Oh, that!' Russ was laughing. 'One of my medical colleagues in Africa asked me to run it for him while I'm in the UK. He doesn't want to sell it; it saves him garaging fees and he knew I needed a car. Don't be deceived by the trappings of a luxurious lifestyle. I really do need the money.'

Lauren looked around at the opulent surroundings. 'So why are you squandering money on a lunch which neither of us needs?'

'I'm not that poor. And I always enjoy a relaxing meal in a gourmet restaurant with a stimulating companion.'

'So you find me stimulating?'

'I enjoy the sparks that fly off you. It's like picking my way through a box of dangerous fireworks. I never know quite what to expect, but it keeps me on my toes.'

Lauren laughed. 'You wait till we have to work together. You'll wonder what's hit you.'

'I certainly hope so. Talking of which, I'll get the bill and we'll go back to the surgery. You can show me the vacant flat before you start your well-woman clinic. Would you like me to come in this evening and help out with the surgery?'

'Your contract doesn't start until next Monday. Before then, all you need to do is settle in the flat.'

'But an extra pair of hands here and there wouldn't come amiss, I'm sure.'

As he spoke, Russ reached out across the table, placing one of his smooth hands over her own.

She took a deep breath, disturbed by the tremor of her own fingers.

'I'll show you the flat. Settle in if you like, but start work next Monday as planned.'

He grinned as he gave her a mock salute. 'Yes, ma'am. Whatever you say. However, I intend to go over to the hospital and check on our meningitis case. If we get an outbreak, you'll need extra staff to handle the situation.'

That was certainly true, but Lauren didn't want to think about such an awful possibility. 'We'll cross that bridge when we come to it. . .if we come to it, I should say.'

They were back at the surgery with only minutes to spare before the start of the well-woman clinic. Lauren was relieved to see that Ruth, bless her, had opened up and was already organising the waiting patients, listening to their queries and checking on the results of the newly returned laboratory tests.

'Have you got the keys to the flat?' she asked Ruth.

Ruth looked up and her eyes moved to the new doctor, standing beside Lauren. She gave him an engaging smile.

'Going to move in, are you, Dr Harvey? You'll find everything clean and aired up there. I got the cleaner to work on it only a few days ago. I must have known you were going to take it. Now, if there's anything you need you only have to pick up the phone and——'

'Yes, thank you, Ruth,' Lauren put in hastily, casting her eyes around the waiting patients. 'I'll be back in a few minutes as soon as I've showed Dr Harvey around the flat.'

As they negotiated the ancient outside staircase, Lauren explained that the original building was over two hundred years old.

'The garage used to be the stable block and this staircase led to an old barn, where, presumably, they kept the hay for the horses. My grandfather sold off the last of the horses when he bought his first car in the 1920s, and then he had the barn converted into a flat so that he could keep an eye on his junior doctors.'

'Just as you'll be keeping an eye on me, I expect.'

Lauren was opening the thick, brass-studded oak door. It creaked on its hinges as she stepped over the threshold. For a brief moment she felt the heat of Russ's breath on the back of her neck and at the same time there was a tingling sensation running down her spine. All of a sudden, she felt the urge to turn round and touch those taunting, sexy lips. Just a touch to see what they felt like. . .nothing that would lead on to anything. . .

'It's a bit chilly in here,' she said, quickly. 'I'll show you how to work the gas boiler in the kitchen; there are thermostats on the radiators. This, of course, is the living-room. The bathroom is through here and this is the bedroom. . .'

For some unknown reason, she was talking rapidly, feeling suddenly very insecure up here by herself with this unknown stranger. . .this man who was rousing all sorts of unwanted feelings.

He walked across and put both hands on the white cotton counterpane of the double bed, pressing his long tapering fingers into the folk weave. Then he turned and bounced on the bed, his face creased with a suggestive grin.

'I always like to test the goods before I buy. This'll do fine.'

She drew in her breath as she met his challenging stare. He was standing on the fluffy bedside mat that Aunt Maud had made. He looked so out of place, his tall frame stooping to avoid banging his head on the low wooden rafters that had been part of the original barn.

'Don't you want to look round the kitchen or. . .?'

'Priorities; I've seen all I need to see. So long as I've got a good bed, that's all that matters.'

As Russ turned and gave a final smoothing of the rustic counterpane he was thinking how enjoyable it was to get this impossibly frigid girl out of her familiar territory. Bring her up to a man's lair and she was petrified. He felt sorry for her; he really felt as if he'd like to help her somehow. . .not try to get her into bed or anything like that. . .but then again. . .

He turned to take a good look at the woman who was hellbent on asserting her position as senior doctor in this setup. He had to admit to himself that she was a fascinating creature—a bundle of nerves but an engaging personality when you bothered to chip away the jagged edges. She had such unusually striking hazel eyes. He wondered if she was aware that she had beautiful teeth. Probably not, otherwise she would have accentuated the fact with a coral-coloured lip-stick, one that wouldn't clash with that awful mop on the top of her head. It was a shame she didn't have her hair cut in a short, chic style, close to the head. He wouldn't mind running his hands through it if. . .

'I'll leave you to settle in,' Lauren said brusquely, making for the top of the outside staircase. 'Phone down to Ruth if you need anything.'

'I'll get my things from the hotel, go over to the hospital and settle in this evening. Perhaps you'd like to come and have supper with me. . .a sort of house-warming. I cook a mean omelette.'

'I'm afraid I can't. I'm on call this evening.'

'So what's the difference between this place and yours?'

'Well, not tonight. I promised my father I'd stay in and play chess with him.' Lauren was improvising and she knew it showed. 'But perhaps another evening. . . if we're both free.' Had she really said that?

'I'll hold you to that.'

He was standing behind her again. She ought to go down the stairs, but instead she turned and looked straight up into those dangerous blue eyes.

He was smiling. 'I've enjoyed meeting you, Lauren. I must admit I was worried I might find you impossible but you're quite human. . .underneath.'

He put out his hands and placed them on her upper arms. She could feel the warmth of his fingers through the thin cotton of her blouse. The gesture was intolerably familiar but for a few seconds she didn't move. It felt so good to be in contact with another human being other than in a professional situation; so good to feel a shiver of anticipatory excitement running through her. She wasn't going to give this man any encouragement, mind, but she wouldn't push him away if. . .if what?

He'd already removed his hands and was turning the key in the door. She rushed down the stairs, thinking how easy it would have been to make a fool of herself. And what a disaster it would be if she let down her guard and allowed this man to become over-familiar.

Ruth looked up from her desk behind the reception counter. 'Is Dr Harvey going to take the flat?'

Lauren nodded, aware of the flush spreading over her face. My God, was she blushing? She hadn't blushed since she was at school.

'It will be so convenient. . .for all of us,' Ruth said.

'That's what I thought. Right! Have the team arrived?' Lauren asked briskly.

Ruth nodded. 'Cheryl's in your room and Lucy is already working with Sister Fiona in the treatment-room.'

Lauren felt a sense of personal satisfaction that her

professional situation was so well organised. She might be a disaster area when it came to her own personal life—or lack of it!—but no one could fault her administration of the Oakwood surgery. She'd had to work hard to keep up the high standards but now her staff knew what to expect. The three part-time members of her nursing team, Sister Fiona Grey, Staff Nurse Lucy Patterson, and Staff Nurse Cheryl Manger all pulled their weight and she valued their expertise and experience. All three nurses came in for the weekly well-woman clinic and, whatever crises in their family lives were happening, they never let Lauren or the patients down. She'd hand-picked her staff from a selection of local well qualified women, when the surgery had expanded four years ago and she'd been asked to set up the new well-woman clinic. Her father had given her *carte blanche* in the selection, saying that one day she would have to take over from him. He hadn't realised just how soon it would be before she was forced to take up the reins after his unfortunate stroke.

'Who's my first patient, Ruth?' Lauren asked.

'Diana—Mrs Fox.' Ruth added the patient's full name, remembering that Dr Lauren liked to have full names to avoid any confusion, even though they knew most of the patients personally.

Lauren looked around the waiting-room until she saw Diana Fox, poised expectantly on the edge of her chair.

'Nice to see you again, Diana. Would you like to come in with me?'

Lauren handed her coat to Ruth and went into her room, smiling as she asked her patient to sit down in the armchair beside her.

'Right, let's take a look at this note from the laboratory, shall we. . .?' Lauren could sense the patient
hanging on her every word. The first smear test had
proved positive. There was a dysplasia of the cells but
it was relatively mild.

'There is a slight abnormality in the cells but, at this
stage, it's nothing to worry about. What I'm going to
do is take another smear and send that off for further
analysis.'

'Have I got cancer, Dr Lauren?'

Lauren looked at Diana Fox's anxious face and
reached out to take hold of her hand. 'No, you haven't,
Diana,' she said, gently. 'But we want to rule out any
predisposition to it. That's why I'm going to do a
further smear test this afternoon.'

'What happens if that one's positive as well?'

'If it's positive, I'll get you an appointment at the
colposcopy clinic for further tests. . .but at this stage
we don't need to consider that. Now, if you'll just slip
behind the screen, Nurse Cheryl will help you undress.'

Lauren bent over her patient as soon as she was
ready for the smear. Diana was holding on to the staff
nurse's hand.

'Just relax. This won't hurt.' Lauren had taken so
many smears that she was confident her patients didn't
suffer at all. Carefully, she slid her speculum into the
vagina before squeezing the handles together to widen
the jaws and give her maximum visibility of the cervix.
Gently, she inserted a swab; the cervix looked healthy
enough, but she wanted to be sure there was no infection, so she would get that analysed at the same time.
Next she inserted a thin flat stick through the speculum
and rotated it gently against the surface of the cervix
to scrape off a thin layer of flat, squamous cells.

'There, you can get dressed again.'

The patient straightened her legs and smiled with relief. 'I didn't feel a thing. Thanks, Doctor.'

Lauren spent a couple of minutes checking on lab reports before asking for her next patient, Barbara Green, to be sent in. Barbara's smear test had shown the presence of a large number of abnormal cells so Lauren knew she would have to refer her to the colposcopy clinic for further investigation.

She chatted briefly with her patient, trying to make her relax by asking about her family. As Barbara chatted about her teenage children it was obvious she was tense, expecting the worst, so Lauren knew she would have to handle her carefully and give her all the support she could.

Gently she broke the news that the lab report was positive so a visit to the colposcopy clinic would have to be made.

'What will they do to me, Dr Lauren?'

Lauren reached forward and took hold of Barbara's trembling hands. 'The doctor will take a more detailed look at your cervix. They've got a special microscope that magnifies everything so that we get a better picture of what's going on.'

'I wish you were going to do it, Dr Lauren.'

'If I had the equipment here, believe me, Barbara, nothing would suit me better. I've been working on the idea of enlarging my well-woman clinic so as to be able to do more sophisticated investigations. It all takes time but I'll get there in the end. Now, is there anything else you'd like to know?'

The questions came tumbling out and Lauren answered them truthfully. It was no use painting a rosy picture when the ultimate diagnosis was still in doubt.

When she was confident that Barbara was coping well with the situation she let her go and got ready for the next patient.

She worked steadily on through the afternoon. She made a point of giving a second appointment to all her patients whether their tests had proved negative or positive. It took time, but she knew that if she told her patients that no news was good news they would still worry until told, face to face. It took up a lot of time but it was worth it.

As the last patient left her room, she sat back against her chair and took a deep breath. The intense concentration could be exhausting and a feeling of weariness was creeping over her. She would have a cup of tea and then try to relax for half an hour before evening surgery. Ian Fairburn would be in soon to give her a hand.

'Dr Harvey is here, Dr Lauren.' Ruth's voice came over the intercom. 'Shall I send him in?'

The question was purely rhetorical. Russ was already walking in carrying two mugs of steaming tea.

'Thought you might need this.'

Lauren gave him a tired smile. 'You can say that again.'

'Thought you might need this,' he repeated, with a wry grin.

'Yes, yes; why are you here?' She took a drink of her tea and watched warily as Russ Harvey pulled his chair towards her.

'Well, it's good to feel welcome, I must say. I've been at the hospital. They're going to contact you this evening. Our little patient's diagnosis is confirmed, I'm afraid. Michael's condition is stable at the moment. But all surgeries have been asked to check on unvaccinated patients. Extra supplies of vaccine are available. I suggest you round up your at-risk patients to come in tomorrow.'

She ran a hand over the top of her hair as the full implications hit her. 'Poor Michael. Are his parents with him?'

'His mother's there; she's planning to stay the night.'

Lauren nodded. 'I'm glad she's with him. I'll try and get over tomorrow if I can.'

'You're tired, aren't you, Lauren?'

She drew in her breath, disturbed by the softness in his voice.

'Yes, I am,' she admitted, hating herself for not being able to fight off the weariness. 'It's been such a long day and I've had very little sleep and now this mammoth task as well as the evening surgery. . .'

She broke off as he reached forward and took both her hands in his. 'You're not going to do the evening surgery. You're going to instruct Ruth to write out a list of non-vaccinated patients for me to contact after I've seen your patients this evening.'

Something inside her was telling her not listen to this intruder who threatened to take over. But the touch of his fingers against hers was so soothing. Was she being weak if she gave in to this feeling of helplessness? And there was another feeling, far more pleasant. She could go along with that sensation quite happily even if she couldn't analyse what it was.

'You're no good to the patients if you're exhausted, Lauren. Believe me, I've seen medical staff work themselves into the ground in Africa and in the long run they're a liability.'

She frowned, still hanging on desperately, but recognising that Russ was right. She had a long day ahead tomorrow, with the extra vaccinations on top of her routine work. She looked down at her hands, still imprisoned in Russ's strong fingers.

Suddenly, he leaned forward and kissed her gently on the cheek. 'Be a good girl and go off duty,' he whispered.

Automatically, she pulled back, snatching her hands away from him. 'You're taking dreadful liberties, Dr Harvey,' she said in a pseudo-prim voice, specifically designed to annoy him.

He grinned. 'I know. I think I'm going to enjoy working with you, Dr Mansfield.'

CHAPTER FOUR

'MICHAEL is making excellent progress. I saw him this morning in the hospital and his doctors assured me that he was now out of danger.'

Lauren cast her eyes around the group of tense-looking patients who'd gathered in the surgery waiting-room for her informal chat and thought she detected a certain relaxation of the worried expressions. A week had flown by since three-year-old Michael had been taken into hospital with meningitis and Lauren had spent so much time trying to reassure her patients that she'd decided to invite everybody who was worried to come to her informal meeting at the end of evening surgery.

Russell Harvey was coming down the steps from the holy of holies and Lauren turned away from the eager faces, frowning at the interruption. She'd specifically asked him not to interrupt her, mainly because she thought she would feel self-conscious if Russ was listening. In some indefinable way he made her nervous, always feeling she had to be on her toes, looking her best—whatever that might be—but she'd had to admit during the past week that he'd been a godsend. The extra work involved with numerous vaccinations, soothing worried parents who had, understandably, brought in children who'd shown the slightest sign of illness, fending off the Press—they'd even been interviewed by the national newspapers—all this had taken extra time.

47

So little by little, Lauren had taken it for granted that Russ would always be around. Ian Fairburn had kept up the home visits, because he knew the patients and the area, and Lauren and Russ had kept the surgery going. The fact that Russell Harvey's contract had only just started had been completely overlooked and although there had been no time to change over consulting-rooms Lauren had simply been too busy to worry about it.

But tonight she was feeling especially apprehensive. Aunt Maud had insisted she bring 'that new young doctor with the long hair' to supper. And from the tone of her voice it had been obvious that Aunt Maud wanted to satisfy her curiosity and prove that she was right in her opinion that he was totally unsuitable for the Mansfield family practice and it was a good thing they were only 'lumbered with him' for three months.

'There's a phone call for you,' Russ said, pausing at the bottom of the stairs. 'Sister Evans insists on speaking to you. Would you like me to take over here?'

Lauren noticed the surge of interest from the gathering. All eyes were on Russ and one of the younger mothers was running a hand over her long blonde hair. There was no doubt about the general consensus of opinion among the female patients!

'Thanks. I'll take it in my room.'

As she closed her door, she saw Russ leaning nonchalantly against the radiator, smiling around at his adulatory audience as he invited further questions.

The phone call was from the colposcopy clinic about Barbara Green. The result of her biopsy showed a severe abnormality of the cervix and they were recommending an immediate cone biopsy in hospital under general anaesthetic.

'We can arrange admission at Chelmsford tomorrow morning but we thought you would want to contact the patient yourself, Dr Mansfield. . .that's your usual practice, I believe.'

Young Sister Evans sounded nervous. She'd obviously been told not to upset Miss Prim, who was a law unto herself.

Lauren tried to modify her voice from the irritated sound she'd made when she first picked up the phone, making it obvious that she resented the interruption.

'Yes, I do like to speak to my patients personally, Sister. Being asked to go into hospital at short notice can be difficult for them. They often have family commitments and arrangements to make.'

The sister refrained from pointing out that there were social services which could deal with that aspect of the situation.

'Thank you, Doctor. I'll leave it with you then.'

Lauren dialled Barbara Green's number. As she waited for an answer she was rehearsing what she would say. The reason she insisted on dealing with this aspect of hospital admission was because so many of her patients were nervous, apprehensive and wanted to voice their fears and she felt it was her job to reassure them.

She was on the phone for about ten minutes, calming the strung-up patient, assuring her there was nothing to worry about, that she would be in good hands, explaining what would happen, checking that there were no family commitments to take care of. Forty-year-old Barbara's three children, aged sixteen, fourteen and twelve, would be at school and her mother, who lived very near, would come in to take care of them when they got home. As Lauren put down the phone she made a conscious effort to stop worrying. She couldn't take on the cares of all her patients. She had to remain detached—something she'd always found difficult.

Going back into the waiting-room, she found a lively discussion going on. Russ's long, lean frame was now sprawled across one of the cushioned armchairs in the middle of the room and the questions were coming thick and fast.

'The chances of catching meningitis are very small,' he was saying.

Lauren noted the way he put the tips of his fingers together and looked over the heads of the patients towards the darkening sky outside the window. She'd seen him doing this more than once during the brief time she'd known him. It was always when he was thinking deeply, and she'd come to realise that Russ was not the shallow character she'd at first assumed.

'The reason for this is because the disease can only be passed on by direct close contact with discharges from the nose or throat of an infected person.'

One of the young mothers pulled a face and Russ was quick to reassure her.

'You can see how this rarely happens; in situations of gross overcrowding we might find the disease spreading but out here in the beautiful English country-side, living in delightful, spacious, well appointed houses. . .' He paused and the rakish grin reappeared on his face.

'I'm beginning to sound like an estate agent.'

Lauren listened to the laughter and saw the further

easing of tension. There was no doubt about it, the man had charisma.

'If there are no more questions we'll call a halt,' she said, quickly. 'Remember, we're always here if you need us.'

'But preferably not in the middle of the night. Try to be ill during daylight hours if you can.'

More laughter. Lauren took a deep breath. Russell Harvey was a typical extrovert. He thrived on adulation. How he ever came to hide himself away in the Third World she couldn't imagine. In fact she couldn't think why he would want to be a doctor.

'Ready, Lauren?' he asked as the outer door closed on the last patient.

She tried to smile, but her facial muscles seemed to have seized up. Oh, God, what an ordeal this was going to be!

'I think I should warn you about my Aunt Maud,' she began tentatively.

'You already have, so don't worry about it,' Russ replied breezily. 'I've seen the old dear from afar as she. . .'

'Aunt Maud is not an old dear. . .she's a highly intelligent lady who leads a useful life but she doesn't suffer fools gladly, so. . .'

'Now I know where you get it from!'

'So don't push your luck, Dr Russell Harvey. I may as well tell you that you're starting at a disadvantage. The glimpses she's caught of you have convinced her that you're either a lady-killer or a man-about-town playboy.'

'Well, I'll say this for your aunt, she's a good judge of character. I can't wait to meet her. By the way, I hope you've noticed that I made the effort to wear a suit tonight. I decided that Ian Fairburn is not the only one who can afford to look the part of staid local doctor.'

'I hardly recognised you when you arrived this evening. Pure wool, isn't it? Charcoal-grey. . .oh, very "consultant". That must have set you back a bit.'

'Worth every penny if it impresses the old dear. . . sorry, the revered lady.'

The gravel on the drive seemed to be connected to a loudspeaker. Lauren was hoping they could sneak in without being noticed, but Aunt Maud was already stationed by the open front door, smoothing down her best navy blue silk dress, her back as straight as a ramrod, her pince-nez carefully positioned so as to scrutinise the intruder to full advantage.

'How do you do, Dr Harvey.' Maud Mansfield extended her arm towards the young man, taking in every aspect of his apparel. Well, at least the fellow owned a suit, which was something she'd begun to doubt.

'Delighted to meet you at last, Miss Mansfield,' Russ said, smiling broadly. 'And what a charming house!' He was already forging ahead, leaving his hostess staring after him as he made a tour of the spacious, oak-panelled entrance hall. 'Alone in my bachelor pad above the garage I was wondering when the rich folks would invite me into the main building. But then I told myself I was only the hired help so I might have to wait a long time.'

Aunt Maud's frown deepened, as she tried to comprehend what this forward young man was talking about. She cleared her throat.

'Come into the drawing-room, Dr Harvey. I've allowed my brother to spend some time with us this evening before he goes back to bed.'

Lauren held her breath as she watched her aunt ushering Russ forward to meet her father. James Mansfield had been impossibly obstinate and irascible since he began to recover from his stroke. It just wasn't possible that the two men would get on together.

'Dr Mansfield.' Russ's voice mellowed and lost its facetious tone as he bent over the reluctant convalescent.

Lauren watched as her father struggled to pull himself to a more upright sitting position in his wheelchair. Elaine Brooks, the middle-aged nurse who cared for him during the day, was standing behind the chair, ready to spring forward if the doctor overtaxed himself but knowing full well that he wouldn't welcome her intervention. The tartan woollen rug covering the doctor's thin legs fell to one side and she moved to tuck it back around his waist.

'Stop fussing, woman! Can't you see I have guests to entertain? Why don't you go off home and look after your poor neglected husband? I can put myself to bed.'

A barely imperceptible frown from Maud Mansfield informed the nurse that she was to take no notice of the patient. Not until he was firmly tucked up in bed would she be free to leave.

'Dr Harvey, how about a whisky?' James Mansfield said. 'Lauren can pour it out for us.'

Lauren moved to the crystal decanter, suppressing her inward laughter as she saw the look of disapproval on her aunt's face.

'James, you know what Dr Dalton said about alcohol.'

'That man is a useless hypocrite and a charlatan.

When we were at medical school together way back in. . .well, whenever it was, we. . .'

Lauren permitted herself to smile openly as she handed over the chunky crystal glasses to the two men. She'd heard it all before but Russ was showing great interest in her father's tales of his youthful exploits. Dr James's speech was still slurred and sometimes painfully slow but the more he practised the more he would improve and there was no better subject he liked to talk about than his supposedly misspent youth.

'Soda with your whisky, Dr Harvey?' Lauren asked, standing beside his elbow in a deliberately subservient pose, the soda syphon poised for action.

Russ grinned. 'Just a splash, Dr Lauren.'

Oh, how she would have loved to turn the nozzle upwards! But she restrained herself, aware that all eyes were suddenly upon her. Returning to the drinks tray, she poured out two small glasses of dry sherry for herself and Aunt Maud.

She knew that Nurse Elaine, being still technically on duty, would decline a drink. This good-natured country woman was extremely patient with her father, but the last few weeks her patience had been wearing a bit thin. More than once, Lauren had seen the strain showing on her face. They were paying her well, and she needed the money; her husband and two of her three sons had been made redundant from their tool-making jobs in Chelmsford. Elaine was the sort of woman who would work all day and still have to go home and clean up after her menfolk. Lauren would have liked to dispense with her services but instead she kept giving her a rise in wages and so, of course, Nurse Elaine was more than willing to put up with Dr James Mansfield's irascibility.

Half an hour later, when Aunt Maud announced that supper was ready, the two men were still deep in conversation, and exchanging anecdotes with each other.

'I'll come to the table tonight, Maud,' Dr Mansfield announced in a truculent voice.

'Now, James, you know it's time you were back in bed. Nurse Elaine has prepared your tray and. . .'

'And she can just unprepare it, because if a man can't sit at his own table. . .well!' The effort of taking such a bold stance had exhausted Lauren's father. He took a deep breath as he glanced belligerently around the drawing-room.

For a few seconds no one spoke. One of the logs from the fire that Aunt Maud always lit in the evenings to take away the chill fell forward on to the hearth. Lauren grasped the brightly polished tongs and placed it back among the smouldering flames, breathing in the evocative aroma. Even now, at the ripe old age of thirty, she still felt brave at performing this task, having been warned not to touch the fire through all those early years of childhood. And here she still was, in the room where she'd sat on her grandfather's lap, the same room, where her mother had lain on the sofa by the window so she could see the spring daffodils for the last time. And now it was her father who was the invalid; but he wasn't going to die for a long time, not with the strong will he was showing!

Lauren turned from the fireplace and pulled herself up. 'Look, Dad, I can't see any reason why you can't come to the table. I mean, for heaven's sake, Russ and I are both doctors. Just don't pass out before we've all had our pudding, that's all we ask.'

'Lauren!' Aunt Maud pursed her lips together.

The old doctor gave his daughter a conspiratorial smile and then leaned across towards Russ.

'Give me a hand with this wheelchair, there's a good chap. No, not you, Elaine. We've got too many medical staff in the place tonight. I thought I told you to go home.'

The long-suffering nurse glanced at Aunt Maud, who gave her reluctant permission. Lauren walked out into the hall with Nurse Elaine, thanking her for all she'd done that day.

'I do hope my father isn't being too impossible, Elaine. You must get very tired, with all your family commitments,' Lauren said as she watched the nurse taking her warm coat from the hall cupboard.

'Bless you, Dr Lauren, it's all part of my job. Dr Mansfield has always been good to me and my family, so I don't mind.'

'And how are you getting on with my aunt nowadays?'

Nurse Elaine gave a wry smile. 'Well, there again, you have to understand that her bark's worse than her bite. Once you get to know her you realise she's got a heart of gold. Bit like you really, Doctor. Goodnight.'

Lauren stood in the hall for a few seconds trying to digest this information. Were people really beginning to compare her with Aunt Maud? She'd always drawn inspiration from her aunt's strong character, always listened to her advice that she should be independent and live her own life, and she'd admired her so much when she was a headmistress. All her life she'd been in awe of Aunt Maud's blunt, outspoken words, yet often she found herself speaking in the same way to other people, especially nowadays, when dealing with difficult medical colleagues. In what was still predomi-

nantly a man's profession, she'd discovered that it was
to her advantage if she was dogmatic and unwavering
on the surface even if on many occasions, she was a
quivering jelly underneath! She was happy with the
successful career she'd carved out for herself but did
she really want to end up like Aunt Maud?

Going back into the drawing-room, she found her
father was still talking to Russ.

'This side of my body is about as useful as a block
of wood at the moment, but I'm working on it. Three
months ago I hadn't got my speech back and now
listen to me.'

'Quite!' muttered Aunt Maud as she returned to the
kitchen to supervise the final arrangements.

Lauren led the way to the dining-room where she
found that Mrs Parsons, their daily housekeeper, having stayed on to help with supper, was now busily
rearranging the table setting.

'I'll sit in my old place at the head of the table,' Dr
James announced. 'Help me over there, Russell.'

Lauren smiled to herself. Somewhere along the way
they had reached first-name terms.

'I prefer Russ, sir,' the younger man said as he
pushed the wheelchair to the head of the table.

'And I prefer Russell,' replied Dr James. 'Now, sit
next to me on my left here and Lauren can sit on my
right and cut up my food. Maud, you sit next to
Russell. There, now you can bring in the soup, Mrs
Parsons.'

The large blue and white willow-pattern tureen was
placed in front of her and Lauren began to serve with
the china ladle. The dinner service had been a wedding
present to her parents—however many years ago?
Thirty-five or something like that.

The steam rose as she took the lid off. Oh, good, it was watercress, one of Mrs Parson's dinner party specials. And there was a jug of cream to swirl on the top.

Such power Lauren felt as she dished up the bowls of soup! Professional situations like working in the operating theatre during her year as a house surgeon hadn't been as awe-inspiring as sitting at the head of the table and being in charge of these simple domestic proceedings. Maybe she should consider marriage some time. . .

She spluttered on her soup as the unlikely thought occurred. Russ looked across the table, fixing his enigmatic blue eyes upon her, his lips twitching at the corner into an amused smile.

'I didn't know there were bones in watercress,' he said, in a voice so quiet that only she heard.

'A crazy idea came into my head.' Everyone was looking at her. 'You wouldn't believe me if I told you, which I certainly don't intend to.'

She saw the questioning look on Aunt Maud's face and knew that she was being over-familiar with her new locum. Aunt Maud was reading more into their relationship than was there. What relationship? They did nothing but spar with each other—usually. . .but there were the odd moments when Lauren found herself drawn towards Russ in a peculiarly indefinable way. She would certainly miss him when he had to move on.

Aunt Maud and Mrs Parsons had excelled themselves with the supper. There was Lauren's favourite, roast leg of lamb with mint sauce, roast potatoes, parsnips, cauliflower and lashings of gravy, followed by the raspberry pavlova that Mrs Parsons always prepared for special occasions.

Lauren was relieved when her father declined a portion of the deliciously wicked dessert.

'Quite enough cholesterol for one evening,' Dr James said, leaning back against the pillow placed strategically behind his head in the wheelchair.

'My sentiments exactly,' said Aunt Maud. 'And now, if Lauren would like to give me a hand, we'll get you into bed, James. It's long past. . .'

'I know, it's long past my bedtime, as our old nanny used to say, eh, Maud?'

For a moment, the creases on Aunt Maud's face seemed to iron themselves out and Lauren caught a glimpse of what the elderly lady might have looked like as a child, all those years ago when she must have raced around this house with her younger brother.

'If you'll permit me, I'll help you upstairs, sir,' Russ said, quickly. 'It could be a strain on the ladies.'

'Well, we've had a lift put in, but it still taxes their strength coping with me,' Dr James said. 'Lauren can give me a hand as well, but you stay here, Maud. You've helped me enough for one day.'

The lift doors closed on the three of them and Dr James put out his good hand to touch Russ on the arm.

'Drives me nuts, that sister of mine, but I wouldn't be without her. Still, it's nice to get the two of you on my own for a while. I can offer you a medicinal brandy, Russell, from the medicine cabinet in my room, if you'd care to stay on for a while.'

'I'd be delighted, sir.'

'Now, Father. . .'

'Oh, be quiet girl. You're beginning to sound just like your aunt.'

Lauren put her hand on the back of the wheelchair, a sudden unwelcome shaft of emotion sweeping over her.

He was right. . .her father was quite right. That was
what she'd wanted as a child, to be strong and forceful
like Aunt Maud. But she didn't want the other less
attractive characteristics that went with her aunt's idea
of independence. She didn't want to be seen as intoler-
ant, unapproachable, hard to the point of insensitivity.
She couldn't bear it if people began to think of her as
that mythical creature 'the old maid'.

A strong, sensitive hand was stealing over her own.
Startled, she looked up to see the amusement in Russ's
eyes. But underneath she could see that he was sym-
pathetic towards her. He seemed to know how her
father's words had stung her even if he didn't fully
understand why.

Deliberately, she turned her hand, so that the palm
was uppermost, against Russ's. She watched the look
of surprise register on his face as she felt the answering
pressure in his contact with her skin.

'Will someone push me out of this damn lift?'

Lauren suppressed her laughter as Russ propelled
her father out on to the landing.

For a moment, she hesitated, wondering what on
earth had come over her. She had actually fancied
Russ in a sensual way. He'd stirred up feelings that
she thought had been crushed out of her all those years
ago. Maybe, if they got together, she would dare
to allow these feelings to mature into something
exciting. . .

She suppressed an involuntary shiver at the unbidden
thought. Where were all these unwanted ideas
coming from?

It took only minutes to settle her father into bed.
He was already in pyjamas and dressing gown; the
male nurse who came in for a couple of hours in the

morning would bath him. And he was as excited as a
schoolboy organising a midnight feast in the dormitory
as he handed Russ the keys to his personal 'medicine
cabinet'.

Lauren stifled the desire to urge restraint as she
watched Russ pouring out generous measures of her
father's expensive brandy into the crystal goblets.

She would make sure that no one would accuse her
of emulating the dicatatorial side of Aunt Maud again!

The last remnants of the fire glowed in the grate. Aunt
Maud had gone to bed, exhausted by the extra work
that the special supper had involved. Before she'd gone
she'd told Lauren that 'there might be some good in
that young man after all'.

Lauren looked into the dying embers of the fire and
smiled. That was a positive compliment coming from
Aunt Maud. She couldn't think why her aunt continued
to call Russ a young man. He was thirty-seven—she'd
looked it up on his CV only this morning. . .for some
reason or other, she couldn't remember. Seven years
older than she was.

She leaned back against the cretonne-covered
cushions, wondering how long her father was going to
keep Russ upstairs. If he did ask her out, she would
certainly go. She wouldn't hold back as she'd done
that first day when he took her out to lunch. And she'd
smarten herself up a bit. . .go out and buy some new
clothes and perhaps call in at that health shop in Ongar
where they gave advice on cosmetics. If Russell
Harvey thought she was going to be the target of his
jokes about her shabby appearance he'd got another
think coming!

She could hear him coming down the stairs and her

pulse-rate suddenly zoomed in the most unwelcome
manner. She held her breath as she told herself she
hoped he would go straight out of the front door. . .
no, that wasn't what she wanted! She wanted him
to come back into the drawing-room, but she'd be
damned if she'd. . .

'Russ! You startled me. . . I'd forgotten you were
still here,' she lied, uncurling her long legs from her
inelegant slouch on the sofa. 'I thought you'd
gone home.'

'No, I wouldn't leave without saying goodnight to
my hostess.'

'Oh, I wasn't the hostess. I can't cook. Aunt Maud
and Mrs Parsons do all that sort of thing. . .'

Her voice trailed away. . .he was leaning over, he
was going to kiss her. . .she could turn away her
head. . .

But for the moment she savoured the wonderfully
sensual feeling that sent shivers trickling down
her spine.

The kiss lasted only a split-second before he pulled
away, and she knew it meant nothing to him. It was
probably the way he always ended the evening with
someone who didn't particularly interest him. Perhaps
he regarded her as an intriguing diversion from the
type of girl with whom he usually spent the evening.
If only she'd turned her head away sooner! Although
she'd enjoyed the momentary excitement of the contact
with his lips, she didn't want to give the impression
that. . .

'Goodnight, Lauren.'

His words cut across her thoughts, reminding her
that she was still staring up into his eyes. Oh, how
naïve could you get! It was only a goodnight kiss, for

heaven's sake! She was being far too intense about it.

She gave him a forced smile as she recovered her composure.

'Goodnight, Russ.'

She walked out into the hall, trying to play the role of hostess and appear as if nothing had happened.

Well, it hadn't, had it? she thought as she closed the door after him and leaned against it. These unwelcome flutterings of emotion, or whatever it was that was disturbing her, were merely because she hadn't made contact with a fanciable man for ages. If she was honest, she'd deliberately avoided being alone with anyone remotely sexy since. . .since that awful time. She'd felt scared if anyone had approached her in a sensual way.

But Russ was different. He disturbed her in a totally different way. The tingling down her spine that she'd felt when he kissed her certainly wasn't fear!

CHAPTER FIVE

SOMEWHERE amid the maelstrom of Lauren's working life, April had turned the corner into May. She glanced out of the open car window and drank in the heady perfume of the May blossom. It was the sort of day that made you feel glad to be alive. . .in more ways than one!

She pressed her lips together, remembering again the disturbing emotions she'd experienced when Russ had kissed her. It was nearly three weeks since that goodnight kiss but, try as she would to dismiss it as trivial, the memory kept flooding back.

She remembered how she'd leaned against the door, breathing deeply to regain her composure, and then she couldn't stop herself from peeping out of the hall window to see him striding away over the gravel drive towards the old stable block.

How soppy could you get? She stared through the windscreen, concentrating madly on the road ahead as she told herself she needed her head examining! These romantic notions just weren't on. They didn't fit in with her scheme of things. . .but she couldn't help feeling the way she did. She couldn't simply dismiss the fact that Russ Harvey was stirring up sensual feelings she'd thought had died forever. And although she tried not to think about it, she couldn't stop herself from hoping that he would ask her out again.

What was it he'd said on that first day when he'd invited her to supper and she'd turned him down? He'd told her he cooked a mean omelette. If she was honest with herself, she wasn't the least bit interested in his prowess as a cook!

For the first time for years she felt interested in a man in a sensual way. Oh, she'd had boyfriends at medical school but they'd never meant anything to her. And she'd deliberately tried to avoid physical contact with them after that particularly unpleasant encounter with Peter Hardcastle.

Eighteen, she'd been, the rawest recruit in the medical school in spite of coming from a long line of experienced doctors. Peter was twenty-four, and in his final year; she'd gone out with him on a couple of occasions and she'd felt slightly in awe of him. She couldn't think why he'd asked her out and in a way, she supposed, she was flattered by his attentions. He seemed so much older and more sophisticated than her.

Both times he'd taken her out he'd invited her back to his flat for coffee but she'd turned down his invitation because she'd thought that coffee was probably the last thing on his mind.

But the third time he'd asked she'd decided to go, purely out of curiosity and a certain sense of bravado. She wanted to prove to herself that she could handle any adult situation, now that she'd left her sheltered home background. As soon as she arrived in Peter's flat a large gin with a very small tonic was pressed upon her, Peter having apparently run out of coffee. She remembered sipping very slowly, detesting the taste of the gin, and planning to escape as soon as she could.

But at this point, Peter had put down his whisky and started making unwelcome advances.

Lauren's hands on the steering-wheel felt sticky as

the unbidden memories flooded back. Easing off the accelerator, she pulled into a lay-by. As soon as she switched off the engine she could hear the cries of the spring birds and from somewhere in the undulating fields above Ongar she heard her first cuckoo.

She leaned back against the driving seat as she reflected that twelve years ago she'd been such a naïve, trusting girl. She'd been way out of her league with Peter. She'd hated those awful brutal lips, the glazed look on his face, the sweaty hands hands pawing indiscriminatingly all over her. Beads of sweat broke out on her forehead as she remembered how she'd had to fight him off.

'Are you all right, miss?'

The kindly constable's face at the window of her car brought her back to the present. She hadn't even heard his car pull in behind her.

'Why, it's you, Dr Lauren. I saw a young girl sitting by herself in the car and I thought you might be in trouble.'

'No, I'm perfectly OK, thank you, but it was kind of you to stop. I. . .I just needed a few quiet minutes to myself. Had a lot of calls to make this morning.'

She turned on the ignition and with a forced smile drove back on to the road, but not before she'd noted the worried expression on the constable's face. This was the first time she'd thought that whole episode through. She'd made a point of blanking it out.

Peter was now a well respected consultant in London with a charming wife and four children. He would most certainly have forgotten all about it because he'd avoided her like the plague after that evening. She felt no rancour towards him when she occasionally saw a picture of him in the newspaper—once in the *Tatler* at a society wedding; he was that sort of social climbing type—because he now bore very little resemblance to the medical student who'd put her off sex all those years ago.

On impulse she decided to go back to the surgery for a coffee with Ruth before she went on to Chelmsford to do the hospital visits.

There was no one in the waiting-room and only a few more minutes of consulting time to go. She wondered if Russ and Ian had clashed again. They didn't get on too well when she wasn't there but she was insisting on keeping to a rota as regards home and hospital visits. Ian had agreed to take the lion's share of visits when Russ first arrived. . .in fact, now she came to think about it, Ian had gone out of his way to be ingratiatingly helpful since the new man was installed. He was being uncharacteristically charming towards her, almost as if. . .no, she was imagining it. Ian was still Ian, good, solid, dependable; he knew their relationship was never going to be anything but platonic. He wasn't stupid enough to imagine that she could ever fancy him as anything other than a good friend—was he? No, of course he wasn't!

She pulled her thoughts back to the question of the duty rota, deciding that now was the time to split the visiting work three ways. She would do her share of home visits, which would be no hardship as she had to admit she liked to get out and about and meet her patients in their own homes.

Ruth leaned over the reception counter. 'Dr Fairburn wants to see you. . .as soon as you come in.'

'But I only came in for a coffee.'

'I'll take two mugs into his room as soon as his patient goes.'

Lauren frowned. 'You're getting bossy in your old age, Ruth.'

Ruth grinned. 'Must be catching, Dr Lauren.'

'Tell Dr Fairburn I'll see him in my room. You can bring the coffee in there. . .now.'

Lauren strode purposefully towards her own domain and settled herself at her desk, thumbing through the mail as she sipped the coffee that Ruth brought in.

Ian Fairburn tapped on the door. She recognised the rhythm of the knocks and called for him to come in. Over the years he'd worked with her she'd always insisted he didn't barge in as he'd tried to do in the early days. School chums they might have been, but there was such a thing as protocol.

His expression was thunderous and Lauren took a deep breath, sensing trouble.

'Sit down, Ian. Ruth's brought your coffee in here and. . .'

'I've had a coffee and I'd rather stand. What I've got to say will only take a few seconds. That. . .that locum upstairs. . .' Ian pointed a fist in the general direction of the holy of holies.

'You mean Dr Harvey,' Lauren interjected calmly, trying to defuse the situation.

'You know who I'm talking about. . .well, he's only entertaining a girlfriend up there in the middle of consulting hours.'

'Are you sure?' Lauren sprang to her feet.

'Of course I'm sure. Go and have a look for yourself if you don't believe me. As head of practice it's your duty to see that this surgery runs efficiently and Dr Take-it-easy Harvey has got to be told how to behave.'

He held open the door and Lauren felt she had

no alternative. Yes, Ian was right, it was her duty, wasn't it?

As she went out into the corridor Ian put a hand on her arm. 'And don't be lenient with him. . .your father would have given him his marching orders. Oh, and before you go, I've been meaning to ask you about the Gilbert and Sullivan week at the Civic Theatre in Chelmsford next month. Shall I book a couple of seats the way I did last year? It's *Pirates of Penzance* on Monday and Tuesday. I thought. . .'

'Oh, not now, Ian!'

God, the man was infuriating! Expecting her to think about going out with him at a time like this! Their last evening out together had been so boring. She'd enjoyed the music at the concert but the snack-bar supper had been something she could have done without. The trouble with Ian was that he had no imagination.

She took the steps two at a time, consequently arriving breathless at the top of the stairs. Taking a leaf out of her own book, she tapped on the door and waited impatiently. A couple of seconds elapsed and then came the required permission.

'Come in. . .why, Lauren, I thought you were out on your rounds.' Russ, leaning back in his chair, his long legs stretched out on the top of the desk, looked anything but nonplussed at the irregular situation.

'Obviously!'

Lauren took a deep breath as she walked over to the desk.

'Would you mind removing your feet from the desk? It wouldn't look good if a patient walked in.'

In her indignation she could barely bring herself to

look at the tall, willowy blonde ensconced in the
patients' chair. And as Russ pulled himself out of his
chair and stood up, she took exception to the sardonic
smile on his face, which seemed to imply that he was
merely humouring her.

'Ah, but I've finished my list for the morning. I had
a cancellation from my last patient. Let me introduce
you to one of my oldest friends.'

'Not so much of the old, if you don't mind, Russ,'
the blonde put in, stretching out a well manicured hand
towards Lauren.

Lauren shook hands, painfully aware of her own
sticky palms as she clasped the other woman's ice-cool,
smoothly conditioned skin.

'Dr Lauren Mansfield, this is Dr Gillian Dawson. . .
Jilly to her friends. We were at medical school together
and. . .'

'I was a couple of years behind you, Russ,' Jilly
Dawson interjected, coyly. 'Don't make Dr Mansfield
think I'm older than I am.'

Lauren would have thought the woman to be much
younger than she obviously was. As she appraised the
well cut gabardine suit she was thinking that Dr
Dawson looked ageless. The sort of woman who would
remain slender and well preserved to the end of her
days. Just the sort of person Lauren expected Russ to
have as a girlfriend.

Lauren sank down into the armchair reserved for
patients' relatives, her eyes taking in the changes that
Russ had made to the room. She wasn't sure her father
would approve at all! He'd removed the posters exhort-
ing patients to stop smoking, stop drinking and adopt
a healthy lifestyle. In their place were some bright
paintings and on one wall were several hand-drawn

pictures signed by his little patients. Now, that was a nice idea!

Deliberately she focused her eyes once more on the newcomer and adopted her senior partner voice.

'So what brings you out into the wilds of Essex, Dr Dawson?'

'I'm on my way to Brentwood for a lunch appointment so I thought I'd make a little detour to see Russ and catch up on all the news. I told him I'd look him up when I got back from Africa.'

'Jilly and I were together for the last three months in Africa. She's attached to the World Health Organisation too,' Russ explained.

Lauren tried to shake off the unwelcome feelings that were moving in as she contemplated what being together meant. It couldn't all have been work. And looking at this vision of well groomed sophistication she couldn't help thinking that Jilly Dawson must have spent an awful lot of time and money on herself since arriving back in the UK.

She stood up, trying to quell the bitchy thoughts that threatened to undermine her neatly organised emotional stability.

'Well, I'll leave you two to. . .er. . .reminisce. You must have such a lot to talk about.'

Outside the door she took a deep breath. What on earth had made her barge in on them like that, breathing fire and brimstone? That wretched Ian Fairburn had a lot to answer for! He was the one who'd got her so incensed. He was always trying to stir things up nowadays in between his bouts of uncharacteristic charm. Was he really upset that another man had come along threatening what he regarded as his own territory? He was certainly behaving strangely.

But as she went slowly back down the stairs she reflected that it wasn't all Ian's fault. She'd been. . . annoyed. . .was that the right word? Jealous possibly?

Certainly not! she tried to tell herself, but a tiny voice inside her head contradicted her. Yes, she was jealous of that sophisticated woman in Russ's room. . . but she wasn't going to admit it, even to herself! She had to fight against such a stupid, useless emotion.

Back in her own room, she sat down at the desk and looked through the rest of the post. There was something wrong with her concentration this morning. Oh, well, there was nothing that couldn't wait.

She pushed aside the pile and looked out of the window. A gentle breeze was ruffling the apple blossom. Midsummer would soon be upon them again. Time was passing too quickly this year. . .

She could hear footsteps coming down the stairs and then someone knocked on her door.

'Come in.'

'Why. . .Dr Dawson. . .' Lauren stared at her visitor.

The elegant blonde approached the desk. 'Do call me Jilly. I felt I had to come and say goodbye to you. Russ got a phone call from his sister just as I was leaving so he's tied up. He doesn't know I'm popping in to see you on my way out. I had the impression that you didn't approve of me dropping in like this so I wanted to say I'm sorry if I upset the surgery procedure.'

'Not at all!' Lauren lied, feeling even more disconcerted as she discovered how charming Russ's friend really was. 'Do sit down, Dr. . .er. . . Jilly.'

'Well, just for a moment and then I must be off. It's only a flying visit. . .so many people to see when

I'm back in the UK. Russ must have the same problem, I'm sure. But at least he doesn't have family to visit. I've got so many relatives, all waiting for me to pop in.'

'Then Russ's sister who's just phoning him doesn't live in the UK, I take it,' Lauren said, trying not to sound as if she was fishing for information about his family background.

'Caroline lives in the States. Russ has always been good to her. She's ten years younger than him and ever since his parents died he's taken over the role of father figure.'

Lauren smiled. 'Somehow I can't imagine Russ as a father figure. He seems so. . .how can I put it? Carefree. . .is that the right word?'

'That's how he appears on the surface, but he's got his serious side and, going back to Caroline, he was a tower of strength when she had her skiing accident a few years ago. She'd gone out to the States to start her teaching job and she was spending the vacation in the mountains of Colorado when she had the most horrific skiing accident. Her pelvis was fractured and one leg had to be amputated. She was in hospital for months. Russ flew out to see her and discovered that she hadn't enough medical insurance to cover the bills. He took out a huge bank loan, but he was telling me he'll have paid it off within the next few months.'

'Yes, I remember he told me he needed to make some money. What an awful thing to happen! But how is his sister now?'

'She's made a remarkable recovery and walks quite well, so I'm told. She had an artificial prosthesis fitted above the knee where her leg was amputated. I believe she wanted to go back to full-time teaching but it would have been too tiring so she's got a little part-time job in a small nursery school. As far as I know it doesn't pay very much, but Russ sends her an allowance.'

'Doesn't she want to come back to England?'

Jilly shook her head. 'Why should she? Like Russ, she was born in Nigeria and she has no roots here. All her friends are there. One friend in particular— he's the orthopaedic consultant who's been in charge of her case. Russ says romance is definitely on the cards and he thinks it's the best thing that could happen to Caroline after all she's been through. After the amputation she was very depressed until she realised she could have a normal life again.'

'So, do you think Caroline will marry this consultant?'

Jilly shrugged. 'I really couldn't say. But, even though Russ would never admit it, I'm sure it would be a great relief to him if he didn't have the financial responsibility of his sister.'

Lauren nodded. She hesitated. 'Tell me, how did they come to be born in Nigeria?'

'Their father was something in the colonial service, I believe, and he chose to spend his retirement in Nigeria after Independence. He was flying from Lagos to Kano in a small plane with Russ's mother when there was a tropical storm. They went down in the bush near Kaduna and it took days to find them.'

Lauren leaned back in her chair, feeling a deep sadness sweeping over her. For all his carefree manner, the new man in her surgery had suffered his share of tragedy.

'How sad! Well, thank you for filling me in on Russ's family background,' she said. 'It certainly helps to understand people when you know something about them.'

Jilly nodded. 'It's as well you know the whole story because I'm sure Russ wouldn't have told you. He doesn't talk about the sad aspects of his life.' She glanced at her watch. 'Look, I must dash. I've enjoyed talking to you. You know, you're not a bit like I imagined you would be when Russ. . .when Russ told me he was going to work here.' She was on her feet, smiling as she went out. 'Goodbye.'

'Goodbye.' Lauren stood up and walked over to the window, leaning against the sill. It was a revelation to hear that Russ had suffered and was still shouldering family c mmitments. To look at him you wouldn't think he had a care in the world.

She could hear footsteps on the stairs again. Hastily she returned to her desk and picked up one of the letters.

Russ walked into her room unannounced.

To cover up the strange emotions she was experiencing she reverted back to her professional self.

'That's the third time this week you've walked in without knocking. Supposing I'd got a patient stripped down to her underwear. . .?'

'Ah, but I knew we'd seen all the patients this morning,' Russ declared, as he sat down in the armchair by the window, looking out across the pleasant countryside.

'Dr Dawson came in to see me. She was a bit concerned that I might disapprove of you entertaining your girlfriends in surgery hours.'

Russ was smiling as he turned his head back to look at Lauren. 'Did you give her a royal pardon?'

'Certainly not!' Lauren said, in a deliberately severe tone. 'I don't approve of socialising in the firm's time. Now what did you want to see me about?'

She leaned back in her chair to get a better view of this man who was having such an undesirably disturbing effect on her.

'I've got two tickets for the Sunday night concert at the Barbican.'

'And?'

'Rather than waste the other one I thought I'd invite you to go with me.'

'You mean your girlfriend turned you down so you thought you'd take pity on me.'

'Something like that,' he replied, with a rakish grin.

Now that he was able to scrutinise Lauren's appearance more carefully, Russ decided he approved of her new green woollen dress, nipped in with a leather belt to show off her narrow waist. And court shoes to match! So she must have taken his advice and bought wellies to keep in the boot of the car for tramping up muddy paths.

'Well, I'm not sure,' Lauren said, in a Miss Prim voice that was designed to quell the butterflies in her stomach. 'I'd better check my diary. . .and who's going to mind the shop if we're both off gallivanting?'

'Ian's on call. And it's time we considered plugging into that new answering service. We're nearly in the twenty-first century, Lauren. We don't have to spend all our time working our fingers to the bone. Leisure, the new commodity that's just as important as medicine and——'

'Spare me the holistic lecture, Dr Harvey,' she interjected abruptly. 'If I'm free I'll come to your concert with you.'

'Look, don't do me any favours, Lauren,' he said impatiently. 'I don't intend to waste the ticket, so you'd better let me know quickly.'

'Tell you what,' Lauren said, cautiously, as she ran a finger down the May page of her desk diary. 'I've been planning to do some shopping in town for ages so maybe I could go up on Saturday, spend the night with my sister and meet you on Sunday evening at the Barbican.'

'We'll meet for lunch,' Russ declared in a voice that told her it was take it or leave it. 'We'll go to the Royal Overseas League. It's my home-from-home when I travel. Afterwards we can go for a walk in St James's Park, have tea at the Ritz and then go on to the concert.'

Lauren shifted in her chair as the reality of the situation hit her. Lunch at the Royal Overseas League, tea at the Ritz. . .it all sounded very grand. What on earth would she wear? And she had to have something sensible to traipse around the park in.

'Lauren? Are you coming with me or not?' His tone was one of mild exasperation as he pulled himself out of the depths of the armchair, crossing the room to stand towering above her.

'It sounds perfect!' she heard herself say. It was as if the voice belonged to another creature, a woman with unlimited time, money, sex appeal, lovers, experience. . . Well, maybe it was time she started living. She'd been hibernating out here in the sticks for far too long!

A light was flashing on the intercom. 'Yes, Ruth?'

'Mrs Dewhirst has brought little Carl in. She's worried it might be. . .you know. . .'

'No, I don't know,' Lauren replied brusquely.

'Well,' Ruth's voice dropped to a whisper. 'Meningitis.'

'Not another one!'

There had been so many false alarms since Michael's admission to hospital that Lauren was getting to the stage where her patience was running thin. But her father had reminded her last night about the fable of the little boy who cried wolf. One of these suspected cases might well turn out to be a real one and she couldn't afford to take the risk.

'Bring them in. . .and hold Dr Harvey's patients for a while. I'd like him to give me a second opinion on this.'

She thought she noticed a change in Russ's expression and detected that he was pleased she should ask his advice. In the month he'd been here she'd come to trust his diagnostic ability. He had the sixth sense her father had when diagnoses were made. She wasn't sure she was quite so gifted in that area as he was. She always demanded the facts and translated them literally, relying on empirical evidence and discounting hunches.

Carl Dewhirst, the little three-year-old, was carried into the consulting-room by his mother. Russ lifted him carefully from his mother's arms and laid him gently on to the examination couch.

'He's been sick all night, Dr Lauren, retching his poor little tummy out till there was nothing left to bring up.'

Lauren felt his skin; very hot; she put a thermometer under his arm. A hundred and two point five. . .just as Michael's had been. But Michael was now out of danger. The risk of an outbreak had been discounted. . .or had it?

She noted the stiff, retracted neck, the way he closed his eyes, disliking the light. There was no rash but that didn't always appear. She would do a routine check, discount all possible diagnoses before assuming the worst.

The little boy was listlessly co-operative as Lauren did a complete examination, quietly reporting her findings to Russ. At the end of this, as she straightened up and turned to face him, she knew she had nothing conclusive to offer.

'Is it meningitis, Dr Lauren?' the mother asked in an urgent voice.

Even as Lauren hesitated, Russ came to her rescue. 'We can't be sure at this stage, Mrs Dewhirst, but my guess is that we're dealing with something other than meningitis. The enlarged tonsils and glands of the neck could indicate some sort of viral infection. I think we'd better have Carl admitted to hospital to be on the safe side until we've made an accurate diagnosis.'

Lauren was nodding in agreement.

Mrs Dewhirst seemed relieved that Carl was going to be taken to hospital and required very little reassurance. When the ambulance had left the surgery, Lauren was able to discuss the case with Russ.

'Are you simply playing safe?' she asked.

Russ shook his head. 'I've got a hunch young Carl might have picked up glandular fever. I once had a case like this soon after I qualified and it was baffling everyone. That's why I've recommended a Paul-Bunnell reaction test as soon as he's admitted. In case you haven't come across this one, I'll explain. That's the test where we take a blood sample and examine the white corpuscles. If they're abnormal we then examine the blood serum for antibodies, testing it out with a small quantity of sheep's blood. If the serum causes the red cells of sheep's blood to agglutinate—in other words clump together—this is known as the Paul

Bunnell reaction. If we do get a positive agglutin reaction, the diagnosis will be confirmed.'

Lauren was surprised to find that she didn't resent Russ's explanation. She had to admit to herself that although she'd read about the Paul-Bunnell reaction in medical textbooks she'd never come across it in her everyday work before.

'But it could be any number of other conditions,' she put in, cautiously. 'I mean, for example, I could feel his spleen was enlarged when I palpated it.'

'Yes, I noticed that, but then that's one of the symptoms of glandular fever; not always present but often it is.'

Lauren was impressed but she kept her feelings to herself.

'Well, I'll make a point of calling into the children's ward when I do my hospital visiting this afternoon.'

Russ was staring at her with a puzzled look. 'I thought you were going to do the hospital this morning. What happened?'

'Every call took twice as long as I expected,' she said quickly. 'Samantha Marsh up at Home Farm wanted me to check out little Robert. He's a month old now. The other two boys are only two and three so she's got her hands full. She's convinced Robert isn't as big as the others were so I had to reassure her that he's doing fine.'

She stopped, wondering why she had to account for her actions to this newcomer. Why was she on the defensive? He might be useful at giving her his valued medical opinions but she didn't want him to assume some sort of professional control over her.

'Thanks for your help,' she said stiffly. 'I'll be on my way.'

'No lunch?' he asked, with a wry smile.

'Haven't time.' Her automatic response came out before she had time to think.

'Yes, you have. Come upstairs. I'll knock up an omelette.'

'That might be nice,' she replied, cautiously, not wanting to appear over-enthusiastic. 'So long as you're quick.'

'I'll take my time,' he retorted. 'It's bad for the digestion to rush these things, and the hospital patients will wait. They're not going anywhere.'

Lauren settled herself in the window seat that looked out over the cobbled courtyard. There was a distinctive smell about the old white-painted wood surrounding the window frames and shutters that she'd first noticed as a child when she'd been allowed to play up there during the times the flat was empty.

'We used to regard this place as our dolls' house when we were small. It was somewhere to play on rainy days. I always felt cheated when it was occupied. In fact, my small sisters used to stand outside in the courtyard and make as much din as they could, hoping the doctor in residence at the time would decide he couldn't stand the place and leave.'

Russ glanced up from the stove, spatula in one hand and blue and white striped butcher's apron tied over his grey suit trousers.

'But you didn't do anything so wicked, of course.'

'I wasn't allowed to. I had to be the sensible one.'

'Tell me about your sisters,' Russ said, when they were settled at the old wooden kitchen table, the large omelette divided between them.

'Jennifer and Jane, twins, two years younger than

me. My mother used to despair of them so eventually she gave up trying to make them behave and. . .'

'So she could concentrate on you.'

'Something like that.'

'Because you were heir to the throne.'

Lauren laughed. 'Sounds very grand, but it wasn't quite like that. I was certainly always told that my father had hoped for a boy to carry on the family tradition. But I thought long and hard before I chose medicine for myself. I wasn't going to be pushed into a career if it wasn't what I wanted. I told my parents I wanted time to work out for myself what I wanted to do. Of course they were thrilled when I announced that I felt a medical career was right for me and yes, I would join the Mansfield medical practice.'

'But wasn't there anything you'd rather have done?'

Lauren shook her head. 'No, I don't think I would have been any good at anything else. I like music; I play the piano. . .but I'd never have been a professional.'

She broke off, feeling that the interrogation into her private life had gone far enough. 'This omelette is delicious. Where did you learn to cook like this?'

'Oh, a bachelor has to survive somehow.'

'Didn't you ever think of marrying?'

Russ hesitated, putting down his fork and placing the tips of his fingers together in what Lauren knew was his 'thoughtful' pose. 'Yes, I thought about it. . . but that's as far as it went. Never met the right girl, I suppose. Lots of girlfriends over the years; I enjoyed being with every one of them but I just didn't want to tie myself down. I love being free to travel. . .to pick up and move on at a moment's notice. You can't do that with a wife and children.'

She noted the huskiness in his voice. For all his glib, free and easy manner, he was a man who felt very deeply. She found herself fighting against an overwhelming desire to reach out and touch him, to run her hands through his unruly hair, and the thought sent fluid shivers running through her. It was almost as if she were melting inside. . .an anatomically impossible situation!

She clenched her hands together until the knuckles turned white. 'I hope you won't pick up and move on before you've finished your three-month contract,' she said in a prim voice.

He laughed. 'I wouldn't dare. You'd sue me for breach of contract. I know your type.'

'Do you?'

For a moment their eyes met. Russ's expression was tender, belying his gruff words.

'You don't know me at all,' Lauren said, amazed at her own boldness. It was as if a demon was taking possession of her larynx, forming words that had nothing to do with her.

'Then we'd better take care of that,' he said, softly.

She watched, mesmerised, as he stood up and walked around to her side of the table, his hands reaching out to take hold of hers. He was pulling her to her feet, his arms wrapping themselves around her in a sensual embrace that accelerated the melting process going on inside her to the extent that she thought her legs would collapse underneath her. But it would have been impossible to faint. Russ's strong arms were holding her up, all the while that his hands caressed her spine. His lips were touching hers, hovering, barely making contact, teasing her, so that she gave a sigh of relief when they formed a kiss.

She held her breath, apprehensive but stimulated at the same time. How would she cope if he wanted to take her to bed? He was a sophisticated man of the world and here she was alone with him in his flat. . . and loving every minute!

As he pulled himself away, she felt a profound sense of disappointment.

Suddenly, he put his hands back on her arms. She welcomed the feeling of excitement that was sweeping over her again and relaxed against him, wondering if he'd sensed the change in her mood. She'd been so tense initially that he was probably apprehensive about kissing her but now maybe he could feel that she was ready to melt into his arms.

But as he bent his head towards her she heard footsteps on the stone stairs outside.

She felt something akin to blind panic. Whatever had possessed her to get into such a compromising situation?

No one must see her like this! It would ruin her reputation: she, the doctor's daughter, now the senior partner, deliberately going up to the locum's flat! She pulled away, moving across the room into the kitchen. She could hear Russ speaking to Ruth at the top of the stairs but she couldn't hear what was being said.

When she finally emerged, Russ was sitting in the window seat. He patted the cushion beside him.

She hesitated but only for a moment.

As she sat down, smoothing her hands over her dress, she looked up at Russ but he seemed to be deliberately avoiding her eyes.

'Ruth came to say the hospital had phoned to see if you were going in this afternoon. I said that you were.'

'I can't think why Ruth couldn't have put the call through here.'

He gave her a deliberately suggestive grin. 'I think she wanted to know what we were up to.'

Lauren counteracted with a prim smile. 'And we weren't up to anything, were we?'

'Merely getting to know each other,' he said, in a calm, matter-of-fact tone.

She stood up and walked over to look in the mirror over the old stone fireplace. 'I'd better do something about my face.'

'It doesn't look any worse than usual.' He ducked as she aimed a cushion at his head. 'You could try putting some powder on your nose. It might stop the patients thinking you're Rudolph the Red-nosed Reindeer.'

'You are the most insufferably rude man I have ever had the misfortune to encounter. Pass my shoulder-bag. Somewhere inside there's a powder compact that Jennifer bought me one Christmas. I found it the other day and thought I might have a go.'

Carefully, she powdered her nose before tracing the outline of her lips and filling them in.

'Careful, Dr Lauren. No one will be able to recognise you. The patients will think you've come to the wrong hospital.'

'Oh, very funny! Ha, ha,' she said, snapping shut her bag and making for the door.

As she hurried down the stone staircase she realised she resented Russ's remarks about her personal appearance more than she cared to admit. Maybe it wouldn't be a bad idea to use a little more make-up. . . when it was appropriate. . .and she would invest in a bottle of scent. . .a large crystal one as Jennifer had on her dressing table. Her sister would advise her when she went up to town at the weekend.

Simply to put an end to the disparaging remarks and show that high-handed man that she could look good if she chose!

CHAPTER SIX

As soon as Lauren arrived at the hospital, Beth Forester, the paediatric sister, invited her into her office for coffee while they discussed their newly admitted patient, little Carl Dewhirst.

'What made you recommend a Paul-Bunnell test?' Sister Forester asked.

'It was a hunch of my colleague's. Dr Harvey had seen a similar case and he suspects glandular fever.'

'Well, all the signs are that he's right. I've just got a report from the lab and we've got a positive agglutin reaction.'

Lauren experienced a sense of relief. 'I'm relieved it's not meningitis. It seems that my other patient Michael's case must have been a one-off.'

Sister nodded. 'Michael's due to leave us at the end of the week. He's made excellent progress and in a few weeks he should have forgotten all about it. When we catch a case early the patient stands a good chance of recovery; it's the late diagnoses that present the problems.'

'And what treatment are you going to give Carl? Glandular fever can take a long time to shake off.'

'Initially, we'll barrier nurse him in the side ward, even though, as you know, glandular fever appears to have a low infectivity.'

Lauren nodded. 'The current thinking is that it's probably caused by a virus which means it's difficult to find a drug that will be effective against it.'

'Yes, we have to rely on good general nursing care, containing the fever, which usually lasts about two weeks but is often subject to relapses. It's the debilitating effect that high temperature has on the poor little mite. We'll have to wait and see how he copes and treat all the symptoms as they come along. Would you like me to call Dr Pedlar?'

Lauren shook her head. Bob Pedlar, the paediatric consultant, would inform her of any changes she needed to know about. She'd known him for years and had absolute faith in him.

'Perhaps we could do a round of my patients now, Sister,' she suggested, putting down her coffee-cup. Beth Forester was an excellent sister but she could talk the hind leg off a donkey if she wasn't busy on the ward! A woman in her mid-forties, she'd been paediatric sister for as long as Lauren could remember. Strong, dependable, capable, but time-consuming when Lauren was in a rush, as she usually was on these occasions.

Michael Smithson was sitting at the end of his bed putting large squiggles in a colouring book. His mother was watching him, a fond expression of relief on her plump face.

'He's doing fine, Doctor. Good thing we caught it early, apparently.'

Lauren smiled. 'Yes, you did the right thing in bringing Michael straight in.'

She ruffled the little boy's fair curly hair and thought how precious this tiny body was, this scrap of humanity that could so easily have been lost if the symptoms had been ignored. She avoided giving her standard lecture on the importance of vaccinations, knowing that the Smithsons had learned the hard way. They didn't need a reminder.

'May I see your picture, Michael?'

The little boy looked up from the mass of indecipherable squiggles on the page. 'I drawed a diningsaw. Look, look. . .'

Lauren bent down so that her eyes were on a level with Michael's.

'It's a beautiful dinosaur,' she said, softly. 'One of the nicest I've ever seen.'

She stayed a few minutes more with the Smithsons discussing the home arrangements for Michael's convalescence before moving on to the side ward. Sister handed her a gown as she went in, fastening the Velcro tabs as they went towards the bed. The nurse specialling Carl moved so that Lauren could get a better look at her patient. He was in a deep sleep, his stertorous breathing painfully obvious. A glance at the charts showed that the high temperature was continuing.

'Carl's in the best place,' Lauren said quietly to his worried-looking mother, who, wrapped in a large hospital gown, was watching her precious son. 'You can go home when you want to. It will be a few days before we see any real change in Carl's condition.'

Mrs Dewhirst nodded. 'I'll go home this evening; I've got the others to see to. But I'll be back in the morning. . .and they would ring me if. . .if. . .'

'Carl's life isn't in danger, Mrs Dewhirst,' Lauren said quickly. 'We simply have to ride out this high temperature for a few days. . .maybe a couple of weeks. But the nurses will make sure he doesn't suffer.'

Mrs Dewhirst managed a weak smile. 'They've been so good to me. . .and to Carl, although he doesn't seem to notice anything.'

Lauren stayed on for a few minutes, reassuring the worried mother.

When she reached the gynaecology ward to visit Barbara Green she was way behind schedule but telling herself that it was more important to keep her patients' relatives happy than run on time. If she was late for evening surgery, Russ would cope.

She felt a warm tingling running down her arms, a happy sensation in her head. Even amid all this pain and suffering she was able to switch off and think about that impossible man with affection. . .with more than affection.

She stopped in the middle of the white corridor, leaning against the windowsill as she looked out across the busy car park, beyond the mass of buildings to the low-lying hills in the distance. She gripped the radiator. It was cold. They'd turned it off for May. The spring was really here at last. Perhaps that was why her emotions were all topsy-turvy.

These weird and wonderful feelings she had for Russ were too complicated. She simply couldn't decide how to cope with them. Certainly they didn't fit in with her plans for the future. . .or rather her lack of plans! She thought she'd been fulfilled enough with her lifestyle before Russ came along and stirred things up. She'd never thought she would be so strongly attracted to anyone. But why did Russ want to spend time with her anyway? Perhaps it was simply because she didn't melt at his feet like most females. He probably thought she was a bit of a challenge. . .a novelty, perhaps? Maybe he was tired of the sophisticated women he usually spent his time with and wanted a change.

She moved on down the corridor, telling herself that whatever it was she must keep things in perspective.

Russ would be out of her life in a matter of weeks and she would return to normal. . .but would she? Would things ever be the same again?

As she turned to look at the visitors trawling the corridor in both directions, their faces gloomy and sad, she felt ashamed of wasting her working hours on worrying over her own inconsequential little world. She had a demanding job to do as a professional and she must put these thoughts out of her head.

She was glad that Barbara Green was in a positive mood when she arrived at the gynaecology ward. Her patient had gone through a lot to get to the stage she was at now. First the positive smear test, followed by the cone biopsy that had revealed extensive dysplasia. A large section of affected tissue had been removed but a hysterectomy had been advised. Lauren remembered counselling Barbara about this only ten days ago.

'You've got three healthy children, Barbara, and you've decided you don't want any more. When you had the cone biopsy, they removed a large section of affected tissue. There's a chance that this might not be the end of the matter, so a hysterectomy would make doubly sure.'

'What would you do if you were me, Doctor?'

The inevitable question had been fired at Lauren and she'd answered, truthfully, that she would go ahead and have the hysterectomy.

Now, as she surveyed her happy patient, sitting in an armchair beside her bed, surrounded by vases of spring flowers, Lauren knew they'd made the right decision.

'Going home tomorrow, Doctor. I could have gone a couple of days ago, but I thought I'd take the chance of giving myself a bit of a rest.'

'Quite right, Barbara. You've had a worrying time. You ought to pamper yourself a bit.'

As Lauren drove back trying desperately to beat the traffic so as to be on time for evening surgery, she told herself that she would take her own advice for once. She would pamper herself before the weekend. . .before her day with Russ. She eased her foot off the accelerator.

Her new shoes were definitely a bit tight, but perhaps that was because she wasn't used to confining her feet into well fitted shoes. What had the shop assistant called them? Sculpted, that was the word! And she'd matched them with the exact shade of the dress she'd bought at Debenham's in Chelmsford. She wondered if Russ had even noticed. Probably not. He was good at pointing out the clothes he didn't like but she was still waiting for him to compliment her on her new regalia. . .not that she really cared what he thought, she told herself, quickly. She was doing this for her own self-esteem, so that she would feel proud of the way she looked. . .it would make her feel good about herself. Yes, that was why she was doing it.

She decided that as part of her weekend pampering she would go to that beauty parlour in Knightsbridge with Jennifer and have the full treatment. They even had a hairdressing department. She took one hand off the steering-wheel and smoothed her hair back from her forehead. That would make Dr Smugly Smooth Russell Harvey sit up and take notice if she had her hair cut! She wasn't going to suffer his disparaging remarks any longer. She could look as good as any other professional woman he might want to compare her with. It was simply that she hadn't found the time to pamper herself before and new clothes had been way down on her list of priorities. But with a bit of time and money she could transform herself.

'If Madame would care to come this way. . .'

Lauren took a deep breath as she followed the white-coated young man through a labyrinth of potted plants. After more than two hours in this beauty salon, she'd decided it resembled an exclusive medical clinic, except that she felt like a fish out of water here, whereas her sister Jennifer was totally at ease, having spent whole days in the place. They were passing cubicles with partly opened curtains where mounds of unwanted cellulite were being pummelled and coaxed into giving up the ghost.

She was glad she was slim—Russ had called her scraggy; what a nerve!—at least she hadn't needed to undergo half of what those well-upholstered women were going through. Her stint on the massage table had been positively relaxing and then the session in the sauna had almost sent her to sleep. The manicure and pedicure had made her feel so pampered, but it was the session with the hairdresser that was worrying her. Jennifer had indulged in all the other treatments with her but she wasn't having her hair done today. Lauren would be on her own for this session and she was feeling decidedly apprehensive about the whole thing. Maybe she should cancel it and wash her hair herself as she usually did. And she'd been thinking about the haircut. . .she even dreamt about it last night and. . .

'In here, please,' the young man directed, with a coaxing smile.

Lauren glanced at her sister Jennifer who was

following on behind to give her moral support and also, if the truth be known, to make sure Lauren didn't get cold feet and walk right out again.

'Go on,' Jennifer whispered. 'André won't bite you.'

André. So that was the young man's name. At least he wasn't putting on a phoney French accent for her benefit, because his vowels were definitely East London.

'It's OK for you,' Lauren told her sister in the hushed tones induced by her opulent surroundings. 'You're not the one who's going to be transformed. I mean, what can he possibly do with. . .?'

'With the burning bush!' her sister giggled. She raised her voice. 'André, I know it's going to be a challenge, but can you do something wonderful to my sister's hair? I mean, you always make mine look so marvellous.'

The young man preened visibly and ran his fingers over Jennifer's long blonde hair. 'Different texture altogether; difficult to believe you're sisters. I think the best thing to do is to cut it all off.'

'No!' Lauren started backing away.

'I mean stylishly, of course,' André said, with a saccharine smile. 'Madame will look the height of elegance and sophistication when I've finished with her. . .'

She was lying back in a chair that reminded her of the last time she'd been to the dentist's. Her head was being gently massaged by strong fingers and the scented aroma of the shampoo was tickling her nostrils, making her want to sneeze but she couldn't reach for a tissue.

And then came the cutting process. Lauren watched in horror as the crimpy ginger curls dropped to the floor one by one. She tried to smile but her face muscles seemed paralysed. Was this how sheep felt when the farmer held them down and took a shearing knife to their lovely coats?

Minutes passed that seemed like hours and then, all of a sudden, she began to see the total transformation and appreciate that it really had done something for her. She could see her forehead for the first time in years and it made her high cheekbones look more distinctive.

André was drying her newly shorn hair. It took so little time to dry. She knew this would be a distinct advantage in her busy life. . .as soon as she could get used to the new look.

'Lauren, it's super!' Jennifer said. 'You look so. . . so chic!'

Lauren ran her hand, tentatively, over the smooth surface of her hair. It felt like velvet! At last she found she could smile and that made the total transformation look even better. . .at least she thought so, but what would. . .what would other people think when she went into the outside world beyond the rarefied atmosphere of this salon?

It was time for her make-up session. A young girl, this time, colour coded her to tone in with 'Madame's unusual colouring'. Apparently, it was difficult to match up the 'distinctively flamboyant red hair' and Lauren's profusion of freckles caused problems too.

'Keep it minimal,' Lauren said. 'I'll never have the time or the patience to put on loads of make-up. Besides, I think it's bad for the skin to wear too much. It clogs up the pores.'

A compromise was reached and Lauren was pleased with the finished results. She finished up buying all the bottles and tubes that Jennifer advised her she would need.

As they went along the road to Harrods, she said to her sister, 'I must be mad spending all this money. I can't understand what's got into me. It's all so. . . so frivolous!'

Her sister gave her a sideways look. 'And about time too. I've been dying to tell you that you should spend more time on yourself. Ever since you took up medicine you've got frumpier and frumpier, but now look at you. . .already you look marvellous! All you need is some new clothes.'

They took the escalator up to the first floor at Harrods and began their search. A cream linen suit became Lauren's favourite choice, with a couple of matching tops. Next it was round the corner into the shoe department where she bought cream leather slingbacks by Ferragamo.

Jennifer was over the moon! 'Honestly, Lauren, I didn't know you had the guts to go through with all this,' she said, as they sat in the taxi going to her house in Hampstead. 'I'm really proud to be seen out with you. I can't think what's brought all this on, but. . . is it a man?'

'Don't be so silly, Jennifer! I just felt the need to smarten myself up a bit, that's all. I'm actually meeting a colleague for lunch tomorrow and. . .'

'I see. . .a male colleague, I presume?'

'Well, as a matter of fact. . .'

'There's no matter of fact about it, Lauren. Even your eyes are sparkling! Oh, do tell me all about him. What's his name?'

Lauren spent the rest of the journey trying to convince her sister. . .and herself. . .that the man she was meeting for lunch had got nothing to do with her desire to smarten herself up. And the more she talked about the impending lunch, the more butterflies seemed to flap around in her stomach.

'My God, what have you done to yourself!'

Lauren stood hesitantly on the steps of the Royal Overseas League as Russ came out through the doors to meet her.

'I didn't recognise you!'

'Is that good or bad?' Lauren barked, irritably.

It had been the devil of a job to get herself here on the stroke of one. The taxi driver from her sister's house hadn't had a clue where Russ's club was. He'd taken her to a couple of clubs in St James's—both being of the men-only variety who'd turned up their snooty noses at her—and now, when she'd eventually got herself to the right place, to be greeted by this supercilious man as if she was something out of Madame Tussaud's!

'Some good, some bad,' Russ said, barely concealing his amusement as he walked around her on the tarmac forecourt.

'If you're going to carry on this tour of inspection, could we go inside? This May heatwave is getting to me and I forgot to pack my deodorant.'

'Talking of packing, where's your suitcase? I know you were planning to stay with your sister last night.'

Lauren swallowed hard. 'It wasn't my idea, but my sister thought it would be nice if we drove out to Hampstead to have tea with her. So I left my things there.'

Russ put a hand under her arm and started moving inside the large impressive building. 'Sounds good to me. I'll ask the porter to cancel our reservation for afternoon tea at the Ritz.'

They were standing inside a high-ceilinged lobby, a couple of uniformed porters manning a wide desk. Russ leaned across and spoke to one of them, after which they walked through a further carpeted lobby, up a few steps. Lauren paused for a few moments to admire the delightful bouquet of flowers that was centre-stage of a spacious sitting area situated at the bottom of a wide staircase that circled upwards to a high domed ceiling.

'Russ!' called a high-pitched voice from the staircase. 'How lovely to see you again. I thought you were still out in Africa.'

Lauren's heart sank as she watched a petite, dark-haired girl tripping lightly down the stairs on incredibly slim ankles and high, stiletto heels. The expensively cut hair framed elfin features encased in flawless make-up. Again Lauren found herself assessing the age and deciding that this was another of Russ's ageless, sophisticated paramours.

'Madeleine!' Russ was now smiling down at the attractive woman. 'Where did you spring from?'

'Oh, I'm staying here while my husband's in the States—you didn't know I got married again, did you? I'm flying out to meet him next week. I'm just on my way to the other side of town for an appointment, but could we meet up in the next few days. . .theatre or something?'

Lauren had drifted away and was ostensibly studying the central bouquet as assiduously as an expert horticulturist. Talk about feeling *de trop*!

'You haven't met my colleague, Dr Lauren Mansfield,' Russ said.

Oh, lord! They were coming over!

'Lauren, this is Madeleine. She used to be one of my favourite air hostesses.'

'Lovely to meet you, Doctor. . .er, Lauren,' Madeleine said, vaguely, before turning back to Russ. 'So when can we meet?'

Lauren noticed the hint of a frown on Russ's face as he shook his head.

'I'm tied up with the new job at the moment. Haven't any free time in the next few days.'

'Well, I'll call you when I get back from the States,' Madeleine said over her shoulder as she hurried away. 'Bye.'

Lauren made no comment as Russ escorted her into a large elegant drawing-room that served as a bar. Glancing around, she appraised the oak panels, high ceilings and long casement windows letting in the unusually warm May sunshine.

'We'll take our drinks in the garden,' Russ said. 'What will you have? Another bloody Mary?'

She smiled. 'I'm off bloody Marys. A glass of cold dry white wine would be lovely.'

They negotiated a wrought-iron staircase down into the garden.

'Oh, it's beautiful!' Lauren looked around appreciatively at the vast, multicoloured profusion of flowers that surrounded the well tended lawn.

The waiter found them a table under a large parasol and placed their drinks in front of them.

'You haven't told me how you've transformed yourself in so short a time,' Russ said, his eyes running over her once more in obvious amazement. 'That cream linen suit. . .it's very. . .well, it's not you, I mean not how I imagine you.'

Lauren frowned. 'It's also very hot. Yesterday was quite cool compared to this. Anyway, my sister Jennifer and I thought it was beautiful and. . .'

'Oh, it is beautiful, Lauren. Oh, please, don't get the wrong idea, it's just. . .so different from anything you ever wore before.'

'Of course it's different!' she said, testily. 'I don't usually spend so much on myself. I bought it in Harrods and it cost an arm and a leg.'

'I'm finding it difficult to get used to the new image. . .but don't change too much. I don't want you to look like all the other women I know.'

'I've only seen a couple, so what do the others look like?'

'Well, most of them are models, film stars, television people, that sort of thing.' he said, with a rakish grin.

She knew him well enough by now to recognise that he was teasing her. She wouldn't rise to his bait. 'How terribly boring for you,' she said, giving a pseudo-yawn.

'Anyway, that's why I chose to spend a lot of time with a frumpy-looking country doctor. But it's very confusing when you change your image. The hair, for instance—how long will that last?'

'Don't you like it?' she asked, trying to appear as if she couldn't care less what his opinion was.

'It reminds me of a golf course, but I love it!' He leaned across and ran his fingers over her smooth, closely cropped hair.

'Don't do that! You'll ruin it,' she said, but she couldn't help smiling as she leaned back against the wrought-iron chair. All that effort had been worth it; all that steaming in the sauna, pummelling on the massage table, manicuring and pedicuring and then the ultimate transformation in the hair salon.

Russ leaned forward and touched her cheek. 'I've never noticed before what finely structured cheekbones you've got. All that hair over your face obscured your best features. . .you're blushing, Lauren!'

'And wouldn't you, if you were being analysed and scrutinised from head to toe?'

He laughed. 'I'm sorry. Let's order some lunch.'

'Something light,' Lauren said. 'Jennifer's baked some cakes and we'll be expected to eat them whether we like it or not.'

They settled for quiche with a green salad, washed down with a bottle of chilled Chablis. The clinking of the ice in the bucket beside the table, the gentle cooing of the pigeons in St James's Park at the end of the club garden. . .even if it was only May it felt like midsummer. She'd never been a romantic in the true sense of the word—in any sense of the word!—but she recognised that she'd been smitten by the romance virus, and the heady fever was one which would take some shaking off.

'Penny for them,' Russ said, screwing his eyes up to shield out the strong sunlight.

'You wouldn't believe me if I told you.' She looked across the table and her heart seemed to turn over. She'd only known this man a month but she couldn't imagine life without him now.

'Are you OK, Lauren?'

'Fine!' she replied, in a breezy tone. 'Shall we go now?'

As they walked along a path through St James's Park, a small, blonde-haired young woman, coming from the other direction, increased her pace as they approached.

'Dr Harvey, how lovely to see you again,' the woman exclaimed. 'When are you going to come into hospital and see us again?'

Lauren stopped still, resignedly thinking, here we go again! The fan club follows him everywhere!

'Sister Harrison!' Russ's face was wreathed in smiles as he looked down at the diminutive, adulatory young woman. 'This is my colleague, Dr Mansfield. Sorry we can't stop; we've got an appointment. Nice to see you again.'

'You will drop in, won't you, Dr Harvey. . .?'

The words followed behind them and Russ turned to wave. 'If I have time, Sister. Bye.'

'Another admirer,' Lauren muttered. 'How do you do it?'

Russ laughed and took hold of her arm. 'I can't help having such charisma.'

'And modest with it!' she quipped, enjoying the feel of his fingers on her arm as they crossed the road to stand with the crowds of tourists outside Buckingham Palace.

It was as if everyone had cast off their cares with their winter clothing. The new cotton sunfrocks, shorts and sleeveless shirts, sandals; the air warm and scented with blossom that almost masked the smell of the petrol fumes as the traffic roared in front of the palace.

'She's in there having her tea,' one young mother was telling her little boy. 'See the flag waving on top of the roof? That means the Queen's at home today.'

'Can we go in and see her, Mum?'

Lauren smiled to herself, remembering all those years ago when she'd asked the same question.

Russ's hand was under her arm. He moved it along to grasp her fingers. She turned to look at him. He looked so handsome in his casual stone-coloured trousers, the smooth camel jacket, the open-necked shirt, his thick hair tumbling over the sides of his forehead.

He'd breezed into her life so suddenly, like a breath of fresh air, and he would soon breeze right out again. She would survive again without him. She would have to! But her life seemed so much more exciting since she'd met him.

They walked through into Green Park, crossing the lake by the narrow bridge, and stopping to admire the vast pink cloud of flamingoes as they preened themselves in the afternoon sunshine.

'I'll bring the car over from the car park,' Russ said. 'Wait for me over there by the road and I'll pick you up.'

Lauren nodded, her eyes still fascinated by the antics of the flamingoes. She would have liked to spend the rest of the afternoon alone with Russ. She realised, with an unwelcome pang of emotion, that she didn't want to have to share him with anyone. The feeling of rapport between them was so good today, so mellow, as if they'd known each other all their lives.

But how would she get rid of these feelings of dependence when he left the practice? She'd never needed anyone in her life before. Was he undermining her sense of independence, weakening her strong character?

At that precise moment in time, she told herself that she didn't care. Russ would leave her and she would cross that bridge when she came to it.

She watched him sprinting off across the grass towards the car park and knew she would have to make the effort to be sociable. Jennifer had meant well when she insisted on meeting Russ, but Lauren would have preferred to leave it another couple of weeks before introducing him to her sister. She should have turned down the invitation! Jennifer could read her like a book and would tease her mercilessly. Too late now!

Her sister was waiting for them in her large Hampstead house, the front door wide open so that she could see her guests the minute they drove through the wrought-iron gates.

Jennifer's husband, Mark, was 'something in the City'. Lauren had never quite fathomed what he did. Some kind of stockbroker, but it was all a complete mystery to her. . .and to Jennifer too. Whenever Lauren had questioned her sister she'd been told that as long as Mark continued to be filthy rich, she didn't mind what he did. Apparently stockbroking was much more lucrative than medicine, and Lauren could well believe it as she once again surveyed her sister's domain. Russ, too, was looking impressed as he surveyed the grandiose mansion on the edge of Hampstead Heath.

'We're round the back by the swimming-pool. The au pair has taken Richard and Christopher for a walk on the Heath, so it's nice and peaceful. Hope you brought your cozzies. . .oh, it doesn't matter, we've got loads of spares. Mark, darling, this is Lauren's latest conquest, Russell Harvey.'

Lauren raised an eyebrow at her sister. Jennifer was doing her matchmaking bit, desperate to get her old maid of a sister off the shelf.

Jennifer's husband reached out his hand towards Russ. 'Glad to meet you. Come through the house while the girls get the cozzies sorted out. You'd like a swim, I take it? Good. Got to keep up the exercise or I'd run to fat. I was forty last birthday and I have to work jolly hard to stay in shape. I work out three times a week at the gym—more if my schedule allows—swim every evening when I get home. . .'

Lauren linked her arm through her sister's as they strolled through the garden to the swimming area at the back of the house.

'Mark doesn't change, does he?' she said to Jennifer. 'Does he ever relax?'

Jennifer shook her head, smoothing back the long blonde hair that fell on to her narrow shoulders.

'He doesn't know the meaning of the word. He regards exercise as relaxation. When he's asleep that's the only time he's still. He simply can't switch off when he's awake; says he's too much on his mind, always chasing ways of making more money. If I complain, he says he's only doing it for me and the children.'

They were going inside the pine-clad changing-room near the shallow end of the pool. Lauren turned in the doorway to look back at the water's edge where Mark was still talking earnestly to Russ about the importance of keeping fit. Peeling off his shorts and polo shirt, her brother-in-law, now stripped to a pair of figure-hugging swimming-trunks, was preparing to mount the diving board.

'Learned to dive when I was three years old. . .'

Mark's voice still held the same strident quality but it faded away as he put one bare foot on the steps. For an instant, Lauren saw him sway and then he crumpled to the ground. It was Russ's swift action which stopped him rolling into the deep end of the pool.

'Lauren!'

She heard Russ's shout for assistance as she sprinted along the edge of the pool, her sister close on her heels.

Russ was laying Mark down on the hard, flat surface, feeling for the carotid pulse in the hollow between the larynx and the large neck muscle beside it, just under the jawbone. Lauren knelt down to check Mark's breathing.

'No respiration, no pulse,' Russ observed quietly. 'We'll start CPR.'

Lauren turned to look at her ashen-faced sister. 'Phone for an ambulance, Jennifer.'

'It's his heart, isn't it, Lauren?'

'Yes; I think he's had a cardiac arrest.'

Lauren knew that there was no time to lose. Every second was vital. Russ had already put his forefinger under Mark's chin, his thumb on top and pulled the jaw towards him, while with the other hand he was pinching the nose to avoid air escaping. As he blew into the mouth he was checking to see if the chest rose. Next, he put the heel of his hand in the centre of the chest wall and placed his other hand on top to press down hard, before letting go. He worked relentlessly on at a rate of about eighty compressions each minute, culminating in two further breaths into the mouth.

'I can feel the carotid pulse,' Lauren said, after several unbearably long minutes had passed.

'Thank God!' Russ leaned back on his heels.

Lauren wiped a tissue over his forehead, mopping up some of the sweat that threatened to obscure his vision.

'We can stop the chest compression, now that the pulse is there, but I'll carry on the mouth-to-mouth till we get the respiration going,' Lauren said, quickly. 'Get your breath back, Russ.'

A couple of minutes later, Lauren felt a movement of Mark's chest.

'He's breathing. . .Russ, he's breathing!'

A loud siren from the front of the house announced that the ambulance had arrived. Two uniformed attendants appeared with a stretcher.

'We'll take the patient to St Celine's,' Lauren said, taking charge of the situation. Suddenly it seemed very important to her that she should get her brother-in-law to her *alma mater*. She wanted to feel the security that her old teaching hospital always gave her.

She glanced at Jennifer's ashen face and realised that she couldn't bear the thought of her younger sister having to suffer. All her life she'd protected her, right from the time she fell off the garden swing and almost knocked out her two front teeth. Lauren had held them in position with her hand until they'd got her to the dentist. Blood had been dripping all over her little arms but she wouldn't leave go of her.

'Come on, Jennifer,' she said, quietly, putting out her hand towards the pale, shocked woman. 'Mark's going to be OK.'

Jennifer started to cry. 'Is he really, Lauren? Honestly? You're not just saying it?'

'He's going to make it,' Lauren repeated, with a confidence she didn't feel.

As she glimpsed Russ's frowning face, her bravado dwindled even further. She shouldn't have been so dogmatic; she should have told Jennifer it was touch and go from now on. But she couldn't treat her own sister in the way she would have dealt with a patient's relative. Remaining professional with your own family was impossible and she wished she'd been spared this ordeal.

But as she climbed into the ambulance, she realised that it had been a remarkable quirk of fate that she and Russ had been there that afternoon. Those first few minutes following a cardiac arrest were critical. If they hadn't been there, would Jennifer have known what to do? Not a chance! Not scatterbrained, helpless Jennifer, crying softly as she leaned against Lauren's shoulder, her tears playing havoc with the new cream linen suit.

Russ leaned across from the other side of the ambulance where he had been organising the administration of the oxygen. Briefly, he covered her hand with his. She looked up into his eyes and gave him a grateful smile.

CHAPTER SEVEN

As THE ambulance crossed the Thames in the late afternoon sunshine, hurtling to a halt in front of the well-worn stone facade of St Celine's Hospital, Lauren leaned across to check the oxygen cylinder.

The doors of the ambulance were opening. Hands were reaching out to help. A trolley was in its place beside the doors, two nurses and two porters in attendance.

The memories flooded back as she hurried along the white corridor, keeping a careful watch on the unconscious form of her brother-in-law. There was the path lab where she'd proudly taken her first blood sample for analysis and been told there wasn't enough. Over there the radiography unit where she'd struggled to make sense of her first X-rays.

'I don't know why you wanted to become a doctor, Lauren,' Jennifer whispered, her hand clutching Lauren's arm. 'The very smell of this place puts me off. I would have thought you'd seen enough of Dad's problems to go through it yourself.'

Lauren glanced down at her sister. 'Wouldn't you like to sit down, Sis? I'll find you a nice quiet corner in the medics' common-room. You'll only get in the way if you come along with us, and I can let you know how things are going.'

Jennifer flashed her a grateful smile. 'That would be nice. You know me. . .I faint at the sight of blood.'

'Excuse me a moment,' Lauren said to the team

surrounding the unconscious patient. 'I'll settle my sister and then join up with you.'

It had been made perfectly clear to her that the hospital staff had now taken over so her main priority was to see that Jennifer could cope. Only just in time did she manage to get her sister inside the medics' common-room before Jennifer's legs crumpled beneath her.

'Here, take some deep breaths. I'll open another window. Now don't pass out on me, Jennifer.'

Lauren helped her sister to stretch out on one of the long sofas, moving aside the debris of medical journals and newspapers. She took her pulse and decided it was nothing serious, merely a reaction to the stressful situation.

'What about Richard and Christopher?' Remembering her two- and three-year-old nephews, Lauren wondered how they would cope on return from their walk in the park with the au pair.

'Oh, Anna has everything under control. The boys love her. She'll give them supper and put them to bed. I'll call her later on when I've got my breath back.'

Lauren returned to her patient as soon as she could. Mark was now in an intensive therapy unit off the main medical ward. Underneath all the wires and tubes her brother-in-law was barely recognisable, but Lauren was relieved to see that he was breathing naturally.

'We're just waiting for the consultant to arrive, Doctor,' one of the nurses told her.

'Anyone I know?' Lauren asked. Some of her contemporaries were still on the staff here but most had dispersed around the four corners of the world. Still, you never knew.

'Dr Hardcastle,' the nurse replied.

Lauren swallowed. 'Not. . .Peter Hardcastle?'

'Why, yes, as a matter of fact. Do you know him?' The nurse was watching her, curiously.

'I used to know him. . .when I was a medical student. He was further on than me, of course. I'd forgotten he was still here.'

She was talking too quickly. Got to calm down. Peter wouldn't remember her. He'd avoided her all the time she'd continued here as a medical student; she would glimpse him at the end of a corridor and he would deliberately turn the other way. Sometimes, she'd wondered if he was afraid she would accuse him of attempted rape. Because she could quite easily have done so, but she couldn't have borne the publicity, the scandal. And he would have argued that she'd gone willingly to his flat.

A tall, distinguished man in a dark grey suit swept into the room, followed by a couple of white-coated doctors. . .probably the registrar and the houseman, Lauren thought. . .and an efficient-looking middle-aged woman who appeared to be a medical secretary.

Could this really be Peter Hardcastle? He was only six years older than she was but his hair was steely grey; he'd put on a lot of weight, and the jowls around his chin waggled about as he spoke.

'So this is the patient. Can someone fill me in on the case history? My secretary will take notes.'

Lauren took a step back, trying to merge with the general mêlée of medical staff. Gratefully, she watched as Russ took charge, giving a succinct reappraisal of the situation.

'Thank you, Dr Harvey.'

The consultant spent a few minutes making his own examination of the patient, checking the flow of oxygen, the fluctuations of the pulse, the now steadying respiration.

'Well, we seem to have everything under control.' Peter Hardcastle pulled himself upright and looked around the assembled medical team. 'Now, which one of you is the relative of our patient. . .er, sister-in-law, I believe?'

'I am.' Lauren was appalled at the squeak in her voice. She sounded like a mouse. She cleared her throat and over-reacted with a voice more reminiscent of a lion. 'My sister isn't feeling well, so I'll stay here with Mark.'

Oh, God, those eyes! Could she ever forget those piercing grey eyes, now the same colour as his hair?

'Have we met before, Miss. . .er. . .?'

Deep breath. 'Quite possibly. I trained here many years ago. . .'

'Not that many; you're only a child. . .'

Amid the laughter, Lauren reflected that Peter Hardcastle hadn't lost his dangerous charm.

'So you were a nurse here, were you?'

That relentless persistence in everything he did! Like a dog worrying a bone.

'I was a medical student, then I did my year in the house before going into general practice.'

The eyes were widening; the penny was dropping. Lauren's palms felt sweaty. It shouldn't be so hot in here. This was an intensive therapy unit. She turned away, longing to run from the room, but holding carefully on to her nerves. No one must see her distress. . . not Russ. . .especially not Russ. . .

'Are you OK, Lauren?' Russ had moved over to her side, putting an arm around her waist.

She leaned gratefully against him, feeling the strong

power of his body transmitting itself through her.

'It's so hot in here. I need some air.'

'We'll be in the side ward if we're needed,' Russ said firmly.

There was a blur of faces as Russ helped her from the room. Murmured voices were assuring her that the patient was in good hands.

'Don't worry.' 'I'll bring you a cup of tea, my dear.' This from the kindly ITU sister.

But not a word from Peter Hardcastle.

He'd recognised her. She was sure of it. Even with the newly styled hair he'd cottoned on to who she was. She'd worn her hair long as a young medical student, tying it back with a ribbon when she worked on the wards. But her face hadn't changed all that much in twelve years and she was the same height, same weight, same freckles on her face. He knew who she was right enough!

Well, that was his problem! Let him sweat it out! She wasn't going to pursue the matter of his unsavoury behaviour now, any more than she'd done all those years ago.

Lauren leaned back in the side ward armchair and looked across at Russ. Outside the window the night sky was lit by a full moon. How long had they been here at the hospital? It seemed like days but it was only a few hours. She was still reeling from the impact of meeting up with Peter Hardcastle after all these years. And she was wondering what Russ had made of her reaction. Because he'd certainly noticed it. He'd been deliberately kind when he first brought her in here, seemingly anxious that she should recover her equilibrium, but it had been obvious to her that he'd sensed that Peter's appearance had upset her.

She was glad he hadn't questioned her about her distress but he'd been unusually quiet as if brooding over the situation, trying to make some sense of it. Perhaps he would ask questions when he felt she'd fully recovered. She hoped not. She didn't want to discuss it with anyone. . .and especially not Russ. It was an incident in the past that she'd tried so hard to forget.

She was feeling much stronger now and knew it would be possible to go back to Oakwood. Her sister had been persuaded to return home to the children in a taxi. Mark had regained consciousness and had been declared out of danger. Rest and medication were what he now required to restore him to some sort of normality. She would suggest that they make a start as soon as possible.

'I intend to have a chat with your brother-in-law about his lifestyle,' Russ said, his words breaking in on her thoughts. 'It's no good patching him up in here if he goes back to his old way of living. He's a typical type A person, unable to relax, always pushing themselves to the limit, and they're their own worst enemies.'

Lauren was relieved to be able to have a professional discussion. It would ease the tension between them.

'Well, I wish you luck. I've been telling him for years to ease off, but he doesn't listen.'

'Talking of easing off, it's time we took ourselves back to Essex. The patients won't make any allowances for worn-out doctors at the morning surgery. Incidentally, you seem to have recovered from whatever it was that upset you in there.'

The final remark was thrown out oh, so casually, but

Lauren wasn't taken in by Russ's tone. She looked up.

'It was the heat,' she said, in a casual tone.

'So you said. How long have you known him?'

Her heart sank. 'Who?' she asked, testily.

'The consultant.'

'Peter?' Her voice squeaked again.

'There was only one consultant in there to my knowledge,' Russ observed, smoothly.

'A long time,' she replied, in a breathless tone. 'It was all a long time ago.'

'What was?' he persisted.

She gave an involuntary shudder. 'Look, I'm exhausted. Take me home.'

As she hauled herself out of the chair she saw the uncharacteristic frown on Russ's face. Please don't ask any more questions, she prayed.

He didn't, but she knew it was on his mind, even while they were taking a last look at Mark, who was now sleeping peacefully.

They walked briskly along to the main door, moving out into the moonlit night. Only then did she remember that Russ's car was out at Hampstead.

A taxi dropped them outside Jennifer's house. The car was still in the drive where they'd left it all those hours before. Russ started the engine. It purred into action as they cruised out into the road. Minutes later they were on the motorway. Lauren tried desperately to stay awake but her eyelids drooped.

'Wake up, we're back.' Russ was watching her with the same brooding stare he'd adopted in the side ward. She looked away, her eyes focusing on the familiar courtyard.

'I'll walk you back home,' he said, quietly. 'I can see you're under some kind of strain so I want to make sure you get back all in one piece.'

'There's really no need. I can manage by myself,'
she said. But her quavering voice gave her away.

She shivered as he opened the passenger door, putting an arm around her waist as they walked across
the gravel drive. She realised that it was the gesture
of a doctor concerned about his patient. There was no
warmth, no sensuality in the contact between them.
The encounter with Peter seemed to have affected Russ
almost as much as her. She wondered what he'd really
made of it.

The main house was in darkness except for a dim
light in Aunt Maud's bedroom. Lauren wondered if
her aunt was peeping through the curtains and decided
she didn't care. . .well, not much!

They stopped on the top step as Lauren searched
for her key under the porch light. At least Aunt Maud
couldn't see them from here! She put the key in the
door and turned to look up at Russ.

She couldn't stand that hard, brooding expression
on his handsome face. Maybe she should tell him the
whole story, confide in him. He was a doctor and knew
these things happened. But he was also a man. He
might think she'd asked for all she got and she couldn't
bear that. No, it was better she should stay silent.

'Goodnight, Russ,' she said, quickly.

'Goodnight. Sleep well.'

Before she had even turned the key he was walking
back over the gravel. Sleep well, he'd said. As if she
could when all her emotions were in turmoil!

Lauren was in the surgery early next morning. She'd
slept badly, worrying about her brother-in-law as well
as trying to sort out her own mixed up emotional state.

The encounter with Peter had been catastrophic. She'd always feared that she might come face to face with him again but she hadn't realised just how much it would affect her. He was her brother-in-law's consultant. How would she cope if she had to meet up with him again, knowing full well that he'd recognised her?

To add to her problems, when she'd arrived in the house the night before, simply dying to flop into bed, Aunt Maud had come out on to the landing in her capacious woollen dressing-gown to ask why she was so late. Lauren had given a full account of how poor Mark was now in hospital having suffered a cardiac arrest. She'd then had to comfort Aunt Maud, who had insisted that her brother be wakened up and told the sad news.

It had been no use Lauren trying to convince her aunt that the bad news would be easier to handle in the morning and there was nothing her father could do.

So, she'd found herself comforting her father and aunt, assuring them that Mark was in good hands at the hospital and that they would be informed of any change in his condition. She also said that she planned to go and visit her brother-in-law as often as her duties permitted, even though the thought of meeting up with his consultant again was filling her with terror.

All in all, she wasn't feeling too good that morning and, checking her desk, she found she had a full list of patients wanting to see her.

She was relieved to hear Ruth coming in early. That was good. She could plug the incoming calls back to the switchboard. And then footsteps came along the corridor.

The familiar tapping on her door. She pushed aside her disappointment as she realised it was Ian.

'Any more house calls?' he asked, striding over to her desk.

'Not at the moment, but I'll catch you on your mobile if any more come in.'

'What about the Civic Hall next month? Have you decided which night we should go? Personally, I'm in favour of *The Pirates of Penzance* but if you. . .'

'Ian, I can't think about it at the moment! There's such a lot going on. My brother-in-law was taken into hospital last night with a cardiac arrest and. . .'

'Oh, I'm so sorry.' Ian paused. 'Well, take your time making your mind up, Lauren, and let me know. . .'

'I think we'll give it a miss this year, Ian,' she heard herself saying, firmly.

'I see,' he said, in a grim voice. 'Well, I'll be off on my rounds, then.'

And as the door closed, Lauren had the distinct feeling that Ian really did see, and probably far more clearly than she herself did!

She heard raised voices out in the corridor and then Russ's unmistakable footsteps bounding up the stairs to his room. His door slammed shut. Most unusual! The two men must have had words again.

The intercom buzzed. 'Mrs Brown, the school crossing lady, has just come in with young Martin Jones. He tried to cross before she'd stopped the traffic and a car hit him.'

Lauren took a deep breath. 'I'll come out. Don't try to move him. . .'

Sister Fiona Grey from the treatment-room was already opening the door, carrying the unconscious five-year-old in while the distraught Mrs Brown stood to one side, squeezing her hands together to try to stop herself from trembling.

'Take Mrs Brown into the treatment-room and treat her for shock, Fiona,' Lauren whispered.

'Dr Harvey!' she barked into the intercom. 'Get down here, stat!'

Russ was with her in seconds and together they examined their little patient.

'We'd better get him into hospital,' Russ said. 'Did you call the ambulance?'

Lauren nodded, still intent on checking out the unconscious form. 'As far as I can tell there are no fractures.'

'I think he's suffered a head injury,' Russ said as he checked out the inside of the little patient's mouth. 'Well, the airway's free, no obstruction in the mouth.'

Lauren handed over her auriscope, carefully fitting a sterile speculum.

'No cerebro-spinal fluid or blood in the ears, thank goodness,' Russ reported after a careful examination.

Lauren was relieved to hear this. Cerebro-spinal fluid or blood in the ears would have indicated a serious head injury.

'Then we're dealing with a concussion,' she observed. 'A temporary disturbance of the brain.'

'That's what the clinical signs indicate,' Russ agreed.

A barely audible murmur came from the little boy and then he opened his eyes and started to cry.

'You're all right, Martin. Don't worry, Mummy will be with you soon.' Lauren had instructed Ruth to get a message to the parents who lived close by.

The ambulance siren wailed outside just as Martin's mother arrived. By this time, Martin was intent on sitting up and going home, but Lauren explained that he would have to go to hospital to have a thorough check-up and probably spend a couple of days just to make sure there were no further injuries.

The surgery was quiet again as the ambulance left. Lauren remembered Mrs Brown the crossing lady and decided she ought to check on her condition over in the treatment-room.

'Wait a moment.' Russ put out his arm to detain her. 'When I woke up this morning I remembered we'd missed our concert last night.'

'So we did! I'd forgotten all about it.'

'I thought we should rectify the matter on Wednesday afternoon when the surgery is closed— our half-day, remember?'

She felt a tingle of excitement. Russ was back to his normal self again, seeming to have forgotten the strained atmosphere of last night. She would have loved to say yes, but there were staffing problems to organise.

'Somebody has to be on call for emergencies and it's Ian's turn this week. We all have to do a weekend and a Wednesday afternoon every fortnight as you know, but he covered for us yesterday so I don't think he'd take kindly to. . .'

'Oh, to hell with the man! We can't keep pussy-footing around him. I'll ring up the answering service and organise full coverage for emergencies on Wednesday afternoon and evening.'

'Russ, may I remind you that I'm senior partner here and. . .'

'Well, you ring up the answering agency, then!'

'OK, I will!'

They glared at each other before Russ's face creased into a wry grin. 'Good, that's settled, and I'll ring up the Festival Hall and get tickets for Wednesday evening. We can call in to see Mark at the hospital first.'

'Fine!' she said, in a deliberately positive tone. 'I'll phone up and arrange the Wednesday cover. . .but first I must go and check on Mrs Brown. . .'

'Make sure she realises it wasn't her fault,' Russ called after her.

'Of course!' Lauren replied, hurrying across the waiting-room that was filling up at an alarming rate.

What did he take her for? An inexperienced junior doctor? Really, the man was becoming impossibly overpowering! So why was she letting him get away with it? In the past she'd always been able to keep her feelings in orderly compartments. There was her social life and her professional life. She'd been able to go out to a concert with Ian and revert immediately to senior partner the next morning.

But her social life with Russ was spilling over into every aspect of their work together, changing all her ideas about protocol, about exerting her authority.

CHAPTER EIGHT

IN THE early hours of Wednesday morning, Lauren's bedside phone shrilled out. She rolled over and croaked out a sleepy, 'Hello.'

It was Penny Grosvenor, the district midwife, worried about her patient, Mary Best, who was having a prolonged labour. Should she call out the ambulance and get her to hospital?

'No, I'll come, Penny,' she said, her brain clicking into action. 'I can be with you in a few minutes and I know Mary is keen to be delivered at home for a variety of reasons. Hold on till I get there and then we'll make a decision.'

She threw on the first things to hand, which happened to be yesterday's discarded sweater and skirt, and hurried outside. Her car was still in the courtyard so she trudged across the gravel.

The light was on in Russ's living-room. Maybe he's entertaining someone, she thought, and hated the surge of jealousy that came over her. As she started the ignition, his door opened and Russ, fully clothed in jeans and a sweater, came out on to the top step waving his arms at her.

She poked her head out of the car window. 'Can't stop now: I've been called out to. . .'

'I'll get my bag and come with you.'

She watched as he disappeared inside to emerge seconds later. She looked at her watch. Two o'clock and he was still up.

'Strange hours you keep, Dr Harvey,' she said when he reached the bottom of the stone staircase.

'I often stay up late listening to music or reading when I've been out,' he said, lightly. 'We'll take my car. I don't fancy cramping my legs into that sewing machine contraption.'

Lauren switched off the ignition, feeling glad that she wouldn't have to drive around the narrow country lanes in the middle of the night.

'Where to, Dr Mansfield?' Russ asked as his car purred out of the courtyard.

'Riverside Farm. Mary Best is having her third baby and it seems like a prolonged labour. Penny Grosvenor just rang me.'

'So why don't you get her into hospital?'

'Because Mary desperately wants to have this baby at home. She doesn't want to leave the other two children and she hasn't any nearby relatives who can help out apart from her husband. I freely admit she has an irrational fear of hospitals and I couldn't talk her out of it—I think her mother had a bad experience or something, years ago. Anyway, I promised her she could be delivered at home unless there were unforeseen complications. She delivered perfectly normally with the first two boys, Jonathan and Jacob—they're two and four. Mary's only twenty-eight and in perfect health so I'd really like to be able to deliver this baby at home as she's requested.'

Russ took his eyes off the darkened road for a fraction of a second and glanced sideways. 'You can be such a softie when it comes to the patients,' he said, his voice full of an emotion Lauren couldn't decipher.

She looked across at this enigmatic man who seemed

to be taking over her life, against all her inner strivings to remain independent. She positively loved him when he spoke to her in that tender voice. It was almost as if. . .no, she was imagining it. He couldn't possibly feel about her the way she reluctantly felt about him. She must keep on reminding herself that she was just a diversion for him, someone so utterly different from all the other women in his life.

The lights of Riverside Farm shone out over the end of the rough farm track where it merged with the muddy farmyard. The kitchen door was flung wide open and the worried husband stood on the step, relief etched on his face at the sight of two doctors.

'Hello, Simon,' Lauren said, clasping the young man's hand in a reassuring gesture. 'Let's go and see how Mary's getting on.'

Mary Best gave a wan smile and put both her hands on her abdomen as Lauren and Russ went into the brightly lit bedroom.

'Nothing's happening, Dr Lauren. It's all stopped. Do you think the baby's OK?'

Lauren felt a pang of apprehension, but she was sure that Penny Grosvenor would have checked for foetal distress. She looked enquiringly across the patient at her midwife.

'No foetal abnormality, Dr Lauren,' Penny reassured her quickly. 'We've got a good strong heartbeat in there.'

Russ, who'd scrubbed up at the sink in the corner of the bedroom, approached the bed, wiping his hands on a sterile towel which Nurse Grosvenor handed to him.

'Well, let's take a look, shall we?'

Lauren glanced at her patient before going to scrub

her hands, and she could see that Mary was perfectly happy to be examined by Russ.

At the end of the examination, Russ diagnosed that it was a case of uterine inertia, which he would rapidly deal with.

'What's uterine inertia?' Mary Best asked Lauren while Russ went out to the car to fetch an IV stand.

'It's a condition in which the contractions of the womb aren't strong enough to expel the baby. So, Dr Harvey is going to set up a drip of a drug called Oxytocin which will stimulate the contractions and get things moving.'

'How long will it take before the baby comes?' Mary asked.

'Well, that depends,' Lauren answered, cagily, knowing that each case varied widely. 'I would hope you could eat your breakfast without that bump sitting there.'

Mary smiled. 'That will be nice. That's what I'm looking forward to, being here at home and the boys coming to see me and being so excited at seeing their new little sister. . .'

'Who said anything about a sister?' Penny Grosvenor put in. 'It's not down in the notes.'

'I deliberately didn't try to find out,' Mary said. 'I wanted a surprise, but we're hoping for a girl.'

Her husband, who'd settled himself at the side of the bed, squeezed Mary's hand. 'Just so long as you're all right, love, that's all I want,' he whispered.

And Lauren, watching the pair of them, sent up a silent prayer that there would be no further complications. She'd stuck her neck out by allowing this birth to go ahead at home but she was sure. . .or rather, she was almost sure that it would be fine.

An hour after the introduction of the Oxytocin the contractions were coming thick and fast. Lauren made a quick examination of the cervix and declared that Mary could push on the next contraction.

As the baby's head emerged, Lauren instructed Mary to pant so that the rest of the head and face would emerge slowly. She felt for the umbilical cord, sliding a finger under the pubic arch, but it was well out of harm's way. It wouldn't tighten around the baby's neck when the rest of the body emerged.

As the shoulders and body emerged Russ placed the new baby on the mother's abdomen, clamping and cutting the cord. Lauren wiped the tiny eyes, wrapped baby in a sterile towel and placed her in Mary's arms.

'You got your wish; it's a girl,' she said, happily.

'Oh, Dr Lauren, you're so clever!' Mary said, hugging the precious bundle against her.

'No, you're the clever one,' Lauren said.

She smiled across the bed at Russ, trying to understand the enigmatic expression in his eyes. It looked as if he was as moved as she was by the miracle of birth. He might be sophisticated and worldly-wise but he still looked as if he felt deeply.

An hour later, after all the clearing up, as they drove back along the deserted road, Russ said, 'Don't forget we've got a date this afternoon.'

'I'll try to remember. Busy day ahead.' If the truth were known, it had been on her mind ever since he'd asked her to go out. The emergency birth had kept her thoughts occupied but as soon as they'd got into the car she'd begun to think about it.

He walked her back over to the house when they returned. He seemed to have completely forgotten the tension between them on Sunday evening when they'd

come back from London. And as she put her key in
the door he leaned forward to kiss her cheek.

'Goodnight, Lauren,' he said, gently.

Surprised by the touch of his lips she turned her
head to look up at him. He was smiling as he bent
forward and kissed her once more, this time full on
the lips.

She watched as he moved away, her hand stealing
to her lips as if to reassure herself that she hadn't
dreamt it.

It was only hours before they were driving through the
London traffic. Russ found a parking space at
St Celine's Hospital marked 'Consultants Only'.

'I'm glad you wore your consultant's suit today,'
Lauren observed, trying to disguise her admiration as
she watched him extricating his long legs from the car.

He looked good in his customary casual gear, but
whenever he put on that charcoal-grey suit she felt so
proud to be seen with him! The thought made her
groan inside. Was she becoming as soppy as her sisters?
She hoped not!

They were plunged into an immediate family argument when they arrived in the medical unit. Mark had
been moved into a private room and was propped up
in bed, his pale unshaven face listlessly watching the
relentless flow of visitors. Jennifer had brought the
little boys to see their father; his sister-in-law Jane,
helped and hindered by her twin five-year-old daugh-
ters, was arranging the armloads of flowers that peeped
out of the various vases.

'I think we need a bit of quiet in here,' Lauren
announced, briefly greeting her sisters before walking
over to the bedside and taking hold of Mark's hand,

automatically checking his pulse at the same time. 'Would you girls like to go off and have a cup of tea? Too many visitors can be bad for the patient.'

Jane giggled. She was a carbon copy of her sister Jennifer but managed to style her hair differently so that people wouldn't confuse them. At the moment she was sporting a short ash-blonde bob which was in direct contrast to Jennifer's long, highlighted, loosely flowing tresses. Her little girls, Christina and Marguerite, had been styled by André at the same hairdressing section of the Knightsbridge beauty salon and seemed like smaller versions of their mother.

'Always bossing us around, Lauren,' Jane observed, goodnaturedly. 'You've only been here two seconds and you're taking charge.'

Jennifer sprung to her elder sister's defence. 'If it hadn't been for Lauren and Russ, poor old Mark might not be here. Come on, Sis, let's take the kids home and put them to bed.'

Lauren kissed her nieces and nephews goodbye. She was very fond of them and they got on like a house on fire when she went to stay with them, but she didn't think Mark's bedside was the place for active children.

'Thanks for creating a bit of peace and quiet,' Mark said, when the door closed behind his nearest and dearest. 'I heard Dr Hardcastle, distinctly, giving orders that I should have complete rest but. . .incidentally, he was asking about you, Lauren.'

'Really?' Oh, God, that squeaky voice again! So treacherously revealing. She could feel Russ's eyes, brooding and enigmatic, upon her.

'Wanted to know if you were married, how long you'd been a GP. . .generally interested in you. Said he might have met you when you were a medical student. If he hadn't told me he had a wife and four children I'd have thought he fancied you.'

'Don't be ridiculous!' she said, sharply, and then tried to change her unnecessarily severe tone. 'Well, now, let's see what medication you're on and how it's affecting you.'

She pored over the charts with Russ, aware that her pulse was racing.

'Would you like me to see if Dr Hardcastle is still around?' Russ asked. 'We could discuss Mark's treatment more fully. I'm not sure I agree with this dosage here. If I were in charge I'd. . .'

'Well, you're not in charge,' Lauren said quickly to hide her confusion. 'Peter Hardcastle is the consultant and he wouldn't take kindly to having his methods questioned. I know what he's like. He. . .'

Both men were looking at her. Russ's expression was severely critical.

'Do you, now?' Russ queried.

Lauren was trying desperately to regain her composure. 'Ships that pass in the night,' she babbled, off the top of her head. 'It was all a long time ago. Anyway, I think we should leave you to get some rest, Mark. I'll have a word with the nurses on my way out and get them to monitor the number of visitors you get.'

As the opening chords of Beethoven's Fourth Piano Concerto rang out through the Festival Hall, Lauren felt herself relaxing again. She'd been tense ever since their visit to the hospital but now, at last, she felt she could begin to enjoy herself. Russ hadn't asked any more questions about Peter Hardcastle during the early evening. They'd had a quiet drink in the bar before the concert and he appeared to have forgotten all about the wretched consultant.

At the end of the programme she clapped furiously with everyone else. It had been a moving and relaxing experience, just the sort of evening she'd needed.

And then they were making their way out through the foyer into the dark rainy night. They drove out of the car park, crossed the Thames and worked their way along the Thames Embankment and into the narrow streets of Chelsea where Russ had told her he knew a little restaurant.

It was a cosy, appealing sort of place, cottagey in style and décor. They ate a salmon roulade starter, followed by smoked wood pigeon, and then Lauren chose a plate of tropical fruits, because she'd never even heard of some of them before and she was curious to experience the new tastes.

As they drove back along the motorway she was glad that they'd stayed on mineral water all evening. . . especially Russ who had to do the driving. It had been romantic enough without needing any champagne or wine. Just being with Russ on her own gave her a heady intoxicating feeling that she found so difficult to cope with.

Lauren could hear the phone ringing as Russ switched off the engine in the courtyard. It was two minutes past midnight. The answering service must have disconnected at the start of the new day. She raced across the courtyard and let herself into the surgery while Russ parked the car.

'Yes, you must keep him warm and I'll come at once,' she was saying as Russ came in.

'Who was that?' he asked, sharply.

'Old Mrs Bentham out at Greendale Farm. Her husband can't sleep. She says it's his chest. She sounded very worried.'

Russ groaned. 'Couldn't it wait until morning?'

'I expect it could but I've known the Benthams all my life and my father would never forgive me if I let them down. He always used to go out to see them when they phoned up at night.'

'Oh, so they make a habit of this, do they?'

Lauren gave a wry grin. 'I suppose they do. Joe Bentham has been chain-smoking all his life. It's a wonder he's still here. You can imagine the state of his chest.'

'Well, the first thing I shall do is tell him to pack up smoking,' Russ said firmly.

'Oh, so you're coming with me, are you?'

'Of course. It isn't safe for you to be cruising around in the early hours by yourself.'

'You're becoming very bossy!'

'Do you mind?'

'Of course I do!' she said in a severe voice, but she suspected that Russ could read her like a book. Why was she being so pliant?

All the lights of the old farmhouse blazed out across the farm track.

'Looks pretty serious,' Russ said, pulling the car up in front of the kitchen window and surveying the illuminated building.

'Oh, neither of them sleeps much at night,' Lauren said. 'I think they treat it as their daytime. The last couple of times I called during the day they were both asleep.'

'Come in, Lauren. How's your father?' Mrs Bentham said as she opened the kitchen door. 'Oh, and you've brought the new doctor. Kettle's just boiled. I'll make a fresh pot.'

'Dad's improving, Mrs Bentham, but how about your husband? You sounded so worried on the phone.'

'Did I? Well, he was having one of his turns, you know, coughing something dreadful, but he's all right now. He's gone back to his room again.'

Mrs Bentham took them through the kitchen into a room at the back that must have been the old parlour. An elderly man was propped against the pillows in his bed watching an early-morning black and white film on the television.

'Zap that thing off, Joe! Young Dr Lauren has come to see you.' Mrs Bentham seized hold of the television zapper and the screen went dead.

'I was watching that! Why are you here, Lauren? Where's your dad?'

'He's taking things easy for a while, Mr Bentham. Now why don't I take a look at this chest of yours to see why it's causing all this trouble?'

'Nothing wrong with me chest.' He glared at his wife. 'Pass me my cigarettes, Mother.'

'That's not a good idea, sir,' Russ said, moving to the bedside.

'And who are you?'

'I'm Dr Harvey and I'm just going to examine your chest. Let's have you sitting up. . .that's the way. . . lean forward, sir. . .mm. . .let me listen here. . .deep breath. . .'

Lauren approved of the way Russ handled their patient. There was something to be said for being a total stranger! You could act dispassionately whereas she was bound up with years of memories in this neighbourhood. The old people who'd admired her in her pram found it difficult to treat her as a professional. She didn't really mind because she'd got used to it.

But as she watched Russ now, she realised how good it was to have someone like him as a partner. Someone to share the load.

Russ was straightening up. 'No more cigarettes, Mr Bentham,' he said, in a firm voice.

'That's what I keep telling him,' Mrs Bentham said. 'I keep the cigarettes in my apron pocket but he wheedles them out of me.'

'I'm going to get you an appointment at the chest clinic in Chelmsford. Now, don't worry, I'll arrange for an ambulance to come and pick you up.'

'I won't have to stay in hospital, will I?' Joe Bentham asked, anxiously. 'I don't like going away from home. They don't let you stay awake and watch films all night. Best part of the day, this is.'

'We'll see what the specialist says,' Lauren said, quickly. 'He'll want to do some X-rays and examine you. So if you give up smoking now you'll be all the more healthy when you see him.'

The old man frowned as he digested this piece of information. 'Well, I can't promise anything,' he said, grudgingly.

'It's your chest, not mine, Mr Bentham,' Russ said, in an even tone.

They went back into the warm kitchen and had a cup of tea with the long-suffering wife.

'I'll make sure he doesn't smoke after this,' she said, pouring out a second cup for Russ. 'And I'm sorry for dragging you out like this. He really only wanted a chat with your father, Lauren. They were at Oakwood infant school together and he loves an excuse to talk

about old times. To tell the truth, I'd forgotten your
father was ill till you answered the phone.'

The rain had stopped when they got back to the surgery
and a recalcitrant moon was peeping out from behind
one of the dark thunderclouds.

They checked the answerphone before walking
across the gravel together. Lauren noticed with relief
that there was no light on in her aunt's room. No
prying eyes straining to see what she was up to!

'This is becoming a habit,' she said, as she put the
key in the front door.

'A good habit, I would say.' Russ's eyes were full
of tenderness as he bent to kiss her.

She savoured the moment again, longing to prolong
the delicious contact of their lips, but in a moment he
was gone, striding back across the moonlit path.

It was no good wishing he would stay longer. She
couldn't hope to hold him here in her mundane life
when he could fly off to the four corners of the earth.
But she could enjoy being with him for as long as
it lasted.

CHAPTER NINE

'GET down here, stat, Russ!' Lauren barked into the intercom.

He was with her in a matter of seconds.

'What's the problem?' He stood in the doorway of her consulting-room, a wry expression on his face. 'Fire, flood or haemorrhage?'

'Shut the door, for God's sake! Come over here.'

Lauren had drawn the curtains around the examination couch but it was obvious that Russ was totally unprepared for being thrust into the final stage of a well advanced labour.

Jane Gregson was stretched out on the couch, her legs in lithotomy position revealing the crown of her baby's head.

'Jane only came in for a check-up; said she'd been having awful backache in the night. Ruth didn't like the look of her, rushed her straight in here and. . .'

Their patient gave out a loud wail and Russ reached for the Entonox machine, fixing the mask over Jane's face so that she could inhale the painkilling nitrous oxide and oxygen.

'Now pant, Jane; don't push yet. . .don't push,' Lauren was saying, her hand over the baby's head, while one finger searched around the tiny neck. She could feel the twisted cord. The head mustn't move at this stage until she'd untwined it from around the baby's neck. Thank God Jane had got here in time! Another few minutes at home and. . .

'There!' Lauren slipped the cord over the baby's head and looked at Russ. 'We can go with the next contraction. . .you can push now, Jane.'

The little body and shoulders slithered out into Lauren's hands. Russ reached for some sterile gauze and swabbed away the mucus from the tiny eyes, nose and mouth before placing the baby directly on to the mother's abdomen. Lauren clamped the cord with two arterial pressure forceps and cut between them.

The baby gave a lusty yell, reminiscent of someone stepping on a cat. Lauren smiled.

'Here's your little boy, Jane.'

'Then it really is a boy!' The young mother grasped her precious son.

'Of course he's a boy. I told you he would be.' Lauren had had a few doubts about the gender during the first scan but later it had been patently obvious that the foetus was well endowed with the masculine appendage. And she remembered how Jane had been so keen to present her husband with a son. What a lovely start to the day! There were certainly compensations to being a doctor.

She leaned over the intercom. 'Hold my patients, Ruth—and Dr Harvey's too. He's in here with me. Any chance of another coffee, and a cup of tea for the mother?'

'Mother! That was quick. OK, coming right up. Shall I call the ambulance?'

'Give it half an hour. No rush. Jane needs to get her breath back and we haven't checked the placenta yet.'

Lauren found herself running late for the rest of the day, but the glow of satisfaction kept her temper from fraying over the patients who'd simply dropped in for a chat.

She was late for her hospital visits over at Chelmsford and could spend only a few minutes in the children's ward with young Carl Dewhirst. He'd partially recovered from his glandular fever, only to have a relapse, so he seemed like a permanent fixture at the hospital. But, as many of her young patients did, he seemed to have adjusted to his institutional life. At the age of three he wasn't missing valuable schooling and was actually enjoying being with the other children now that he'd been declared not infectious.

Plunged back into evening surgery as soon as she arrived back from hospital, Lauren had hardly had time to draw breath. As the last patient went out of her door she leaned back in her chair and breathed a sigh of relief. Maybe she could relax for a while. That was, unless her father was in one of his exacting moods and wanted her to sit with him. He'd insisted on getting rid of his wheelchair in favour of a stick, which meant that he needed even more help than ever before, and by the time Lauren got home in the evenings Aunt Maud and Nurse Elaine were ready to throw in the towel and relinquish all responsibility for the cantankerous man.

The phone rang. She'd sent Ruth off half an hour ago to go to a parents' evening at her children's school; both Ian Fairburn and Russ were off duty, so the switchboard was plugged through to her room. Lauren frowned. Maybe she should take Russ's advice and investigate that new answering service. Being a one-man band had somehow lost its appeal recently.

'Yes?'

'My goodness, we do sound fierce.'

'Oh, it's you, Russ.' She relaxed. 'I was just thinking

we ought to use that answering service more. Last time
we used it they told me I could have a permanent
contract with them. Apparently more and more prac-
tices are using them because they're so efficient and
reliable.'

'I'll get the details before I go.'

'Go? Oh, yes.' She felt an unwelcome tremor of
emotion. The weeks had passed so quickly, especially
since thier concert date. 'When exactly will that be?
I'd forgotten I've got to find a replacement. I must
ring the agency. Will anyone be there now? No, probably not. I'll do it in the morning. . .'

'You sound all in. Come up and have some supper.
I'm just going to fix an omelette, so how about it?'

In her mind's eye she could see him standing
in his small kitchen by the scrubbed wooden table,
a butcher's apron tied over his jeans, a tea towel
draped over one shoulder, his sandy hair falling over
his eyes.

'I can't. I promised Aunt Maud I'd take over from
her this evening.'

Long pause.

'Some things never change, do they, Lauren? It's
time you told your family that you've got a life of your
own to lead. You're not just the doctor's daughter,
you're. . .'

'Look, Dr Know-it-all, I chose to stay here and carry
on the family medical practice myself. Nobody forced
me into it. I led a very fulfilling life. . .before you
came along.'

Oh, God! Why had she said that? She held her
breath. How would Russ take that revelation?

'So what difference have I made?'

She tried to interpret the expression in his voice but

failed miserably. Had she merely annoyed him or had
he divined the real reason for her distress? Did he
know how furious she was with herself for having to
question the rightness of her hard-won emotional
security and independence?

She took a deep breath. 'You seem to expect that
you can snap your fingers and I'll come running. I've
always been totally independent of anyone else. . .'
She broke off, knowing that this just wasn't true any
more. She wanted to go to him now; she wanted to
tell him that she'd never felt like this about anyone
before, but that she was afraid of losing her independence and getting hurt and she simply didn't know how
to cope with her mixed-up emotions. If the truth be
known she enjoyed taking care of her family when
they needed her. That didn't impinge on her independence in any way, but being at the beck and call of
someone outside her family was a daunting idea. That
really was losing your independence! She'd noticed
herself giving in more and more to Russ. . .and actually enjoying it. But would she be able to forget him
when he went away when he was having such a profound effect on her now?

Seconds that seemed like hours elapsed before she
heard him speaking again in a low, husky voice.

'Well, I'm glad you're so content with your life. It's
quite something to know exactly what you want. There
must be very few people who can say that they've
achieved all their ambitions in life.'

'Russ!'

The click at the other end coincided with her plea
for help.

She put her head down on the desk and allowed
herself the luxury of a few tears. Big girls didn't cry

but tonight she didn't feel like a big girl. She felt like little girl lost.

Seconds later she was drying her eyes, blowing her nose loudly. She'd told him she was independent and she would prove it to him. . .and to herself.

In big capitals she wrote a note and stuck it in the middle of her desk where she would be sure to see it in the morning.

'Call the agency. Get a replacement for Russ.'

But when morning came she had other things to think about. From the early hours the phone had been ringing with anxious parents wanting to bring in their children. By seven o'clock there were six children in the surgery. Lauren had explained that home visits were out of the question in the circumstances. Fortunately, all the parents involved had their own transport so they were able to bring in the children wrapped in blankets.

Lauren had hastily called up Ian and Russ, so all three doctors were able to examine and treat the small patients. But the symptoms were so varied it was difficult to give a diagnosis. All the children had headaches, a high temperature and aching muscles. Because of this, all the parents were worried that it might be meningitis.

But after examining each child they were able to rule out meningitis, much to the relief of the parents. The specific clinical signs of meningitis weren't there. There was no stiffness or retraction of the neck; the children didn't shy away from bright lights.

But none the less, Lauren was worried about them.

'It's a flu virus,' she said, quietly, to Russ as they finished examining a small six-year-old boy in the treatment-room.

Meeting like this in a professional situation, neither of them had mentioned their phone conversation. Lauren had determined to play it cool when she saw Russ, but he seemed to have forgotten all about it.

'It's a particularly virulent form,' Russ said. 'My guess is it's the coxsackie virus. It's appeared in other parts of the country this spring, especially in London.'

Lauren nodded. 'I was thinking we'd been lucky to escape it out here. The virus seems to attack the very young and the elderly.'

'The trouble is, antibiotics are useless against it, but try telling the parents that!' Russ said.

'We'll just have to explain that we can treat the symptoms but the flu will have to run its course. Fortunately, all these children are basically healthy and well nourished. They come from good homes where they'll be cared for by loving parents. There's no need to think in terms of hospital admissions.'

'Just as well,' Ian Fairburn said, poking his head round the door and catching the end of the discussion. 'There are no spare beds in the region at the moment.'

'I'll speak to the parents and explain the situation,' Russ said, gathering up his stethoscope and making for the door.

To Lauren's amazement, Ian stood his ground in the doorway, rugby-forward shoulders squared as if about to make a tackle.

'I don't think that's your job,' Ian said, in a low, belligerent voice. 'You seem to forget you're only the locum around here. Lauren and I are partners in this practice. We've know all these parents for years. They don't want some unknown man wandering in for a few weeks and wandering out again. I'll speak to them and. . .'

'Just a minute, Dr Fairburn!'

Russ's voice was icy cold. Lauren had never seen him looking so angry, but she couldn't help admiring the way he kept his cool, whereas Ian was red with rage and positively shaking.

'Ever since I came to this practice you've put obstacles in my way,' Russ said, his voice as hard as steel. 'We're in the middle of a medical crisis and you're childish enough to start throwing your weight around. We'll continue this discussion at a more suitable time, but for the moment. . .'

'Oh, no, we'll settle it now,' Ian cut in.

'For God's sake, keep your voice down, Ian!' Lauren hissed. 'I agree with Russ that we should talk later. I'll go and talk to the parents and that's the end of the matter.'

'Oh, yes, you would agree with Russ wouldn't you? The blue-eyed boy who can't put a foot wrong. We're partners in this practice, Lauren. He's only a locum. Before he came along. . .'

'Lauren, go and speak to the parents and let's get these children back to their homes,' Russ broke in.

She hesitated momentarily, her natural instinct being to object to Russ's peremptory tone. But the patients came first and Ian's tantrums shouldn't hold things up.

She moved towards the door. 'Go back to your patients, Ian,' she said, firmly.

'You shouldn't let him talk to you like that,' Ian countered, but he moved aside as Lauren reached him. 'You're senior partner and. . .'

Lauren went out into the waiting-room, ignoring the flow of words.

'Hello, everybody. . .' she began in a confident tone, proceeding to explain how they were going to cope with the flu virus, doing her best to allay all their fears and explain the treatment.

It was only later, when the waiting-room was empty and all the parents and children had gone home, that she found she was deeply upset by the confrontation between Russ and Ian. As she sat in her consulting-room sipping a mug of hot coffee she found her mind going over the whole scene and trying to make sense of what was happening to Ian. He'd never been belligerent before. It was obvious that he was jealous of Russ; the blue-eyed boy, he'd called him. Was he jealous on a professional level or was it something deeper?

She shook her head and looked out of the window. So confusing! Ian had always been a good school chum, somebody to go out with occasionally, but never to take seriously. They'd never so much as exchanged a goodnight kiss. That was why she'd felt so safe with him—because he didn't pose a physical threat to her. So safe and so boring!

She leaned back in her chair, suddenly feeling emotionally shredded. Coming so soon after her quarrel with Russ on the phone it was almost more than she could take. She was still smarting from the way Russ had tried to interfere, suggesting that she should tell her family she had her own life to lead and. . .

The intercom buzzed and Ruth announced that another worried parent and child had arrived. The door had been locked for the lunch break but she'd opened it up for them.

'Send them in, Ruth,' Lauren said, running a hand over her hair as she pushed her personal problems to the back of her mind.

*　　*　　*

There were more cases of flu to deal with among the local children and then came news that it had spread to some of the elderly people.

Lauren's practice took care of the local residential home and all three doctors were called out at various times of the day and night. This particular kind of flu was always worse with the elderly folk. The danger was that it would lead on to other ailments such as bronchitis and pneumonia.

A week passed and the number of new cases was dwindling. But then Lauren got a phone call from old Mrs Bentham. Lauren was just about to call in her first patient of the day when her phone rang.

'I'm putting Mrs Bentham through to you, Dr Lauren,' Ruth said. 'It sounds urgent.'

Lauren drummed her fingers on the desk, reflecting that as soon as she could get her father to agree to a trip in the car, she was going to drive him out to the Bentham farm. She hadn't forgotten her visit out there in the middle of the night when Mrs Bentham had said her husband wanted a chat with his old school chum. As she waited for Ruth to plug the call through she wondered if Mr Bentham had managed to stop smoking before his hospital appointment at the chest clinic. It was strange she hadn't heard from the hospital considering the appointment was a couple of weeks ago. . .

'Hello, Mrs Bentham? What can I do for you?'

'He's gone, Doctor. Joe's gone.'

The voice was so matter-of-fact, so equable, that for the first moment Lauren wanted to ask where Mr Bentham had gone. But something stopped her. A cold shiver ran over her. She'd heard that phrase so often before, usually uttered by someone much older than herself.

'You mean. . .?' she began cautiously and was relieved to hear Mrs Bentham going on to explain.

'He passed away in the early hours, maybe three or was it four? He'd got that flu that's going around and. . .'

'But why didn't you call me out, Mrs Bentham? You know I would have come.'

'I know you would, Doctor. But you see, he wouldn't give up the cigarettes. They were his only pleasure. . . that and the late-night films on the television. So he didn't want you to know he was still smoking. He phoned up to cancel his hospital appointment. . .well, they gave him another appointment but he didn't intend to go. When he got the flu he made me promise not to call you out. He went very peaceful at the end. . .just sort of slipped away. . .'

Lauren had to hold back the tears as she talked on to Mrs Bentham, telling her that she would drive out immediately and see to all the necessary arrangements.

As she put down the phone, she knew there was nothing she could have done to prolong Mr Bentham's life, given the bad state of his lungs. Once the flu virus had taken hold he would have been unable to fight it off.

Ruth agreed to phone round and cancel her later patients and the patients already in the waiting-room were given the option of waiting till Lauren got back from the Bentham farm or making another appointment.

Russ had already left to do the house calls. Lauren knew he would be saddened by the news. He'd taken a liking to Joe Bentham that night when they'd gone out there together.

As she searched for the papers she would need, she came across the note she'd written to herself about getting a replacement for Russ.

She would do it later today. . .she really would!

CHAPTER TEN

'I THINK we should get a permanent partner,' James Mansfield told his daughter firmly. 'I can't see myself getting back into harness in the near future—if at all. We've got to be realistic. I ought to retire and hand over the reins completely.'

Lauren looked across the supper table at her father and, seeing the pain behind his eyes, she knew how much it had cost him to make this admission. He'd been fighting against the inevitable ever since his stroke, and she'd deliberately refrained from pointing out the obvious, knowing that it must appear to be his decision.

'Well, if that's what you want, Dad.'

'How about Russell Harvey?' Aunt Maud narrowed her eyes shrewdly as she directed her gaze on Lauren. 'I know I didn't think much of him when he first arrived but he's rather grown on me from what I've seen lately. Incidentally, isn't it time you invited him over for supper again? I hate to think of the poor young man cooking for himself every evening in that poky little flat.'

'Oh, he often goes out for meals,' Lauren said, feeling a miserable twinge gnawing away inside her.

If only she hadn't turned him down when he'd invited her up to his flat for supper that night! And if only she hadn't made it clear to him in the days that followed that she resented his brusque words on the phone. She'd seen him zooming out most evenings in his flashy car, going heaven knew where. Alone when he went out and alone when he came back, but it was the in-between bit she didn't like to think about.

'Well, ask him over one evening,' Aunt Maud persisted. 'And find out if he's interested in staying on.'

'Thank you, Maud,' Dr James said, brusquely. 'Lauren is in charge of staffing arrangements now, so no doubt she's got everything under control.'

If only she had! 'I'll have to change the job specification,' Lauren said, quickly. If the truth were known, she'd been hovering and dithering—most unlike her!—about what to do. She'd even considered asking Russ outright what his plans were. But she couldn't forget the phone call that evening. Russ shouldn't have spoken to her like that. She carried on the medical practice because she wanted to; she spent time with her family because she chose to. . .and also because it's expected of you, said the little voice inside her head.

Russ was right when he pointed out that she was still giving so much of herself to her family. She'd worked so hard to be independent in every other way, but in matters of family the situation was still the same as when she was a child. But it had hurt when he pointed this out. That was why she'd protested so much that she didn't need anybody!

She'd had two weeks to get over her indignation, two weeks in which she'd hardly had time to speak to Russ about anything except work. It was getting so near the end of his contract and she hadn't replaced him.

The couple of temporary locums that the agency had come up with were far too inexperienced. She'd glanced through their CVs and turned them both down.

'I'll go and see him,' she announced, throwing down her starched white napkin and pushing back her chair.

Aunt Maud frowned as the chair legs grated on the polished floor. She knew she should have lifted the chair. How many times had she been told. . .? Oh, to hell with it! She marched over to the door before the predictable recriminations set in.

'At this hour?' Maud Mansfield looked over the top of her pince-nez, gesturing towards the antique grandfather clock, which, as if on cue, began the first of its nine chimes.

Lauren turned. 'You mean I shouldn't be seen entering a man's apartment after dark? Aunt Maud, I'm thirty years old. I'm not a child.'

'There's no need to take that tone with me. You're a woman. . .and a Mansfield.'

'Oh, spare me the lecture on the honour of the family. . .'

'Lauren, you will apologise to your aunt!' Dr James's voice was harsh, but there was the glimmer of a twinkle behind his eyes. He enjoyed these sparring matches around the table. They were becoming more and more frequent lately.

Lauren swallowed. 'I'm sorry, Aunt Maud. I shouldn't have lost my temper with you. I've had a hard day.'

On impulse, she went back to the table, put her hands on her aunt's frail shoulders and kissed the soft down of her cheek. The familiar smell of lavender wafted over her nostrils.

'Well, don't forget to put your coat on. I know it's nearly July, but it's chilly when the sun goes down.'

She'd escaped! As Lauren's feet clattered on the old cobblestones of the courtyard, she felt like a teenager

being let out with a late pass. How could she ever shake
off the family shackles? All that emotional blackmail!
Other girls seemed to manage it, but her circumstances
were different. It was like living over the family shop.
She was part and parcel of the whole setup and. . .

The door at the top of the stairs was opening. He
was coming down the steps.

'Well, hello, stranger. What are you doing prowling
about at this late hour? Isn't it past your bedtime?'

'I couldn't sleep so I came to borrow some cocoa.'
She stood uncertainly at the foot of the stairs. From
somewhere overhead she heard the flapping of tiny
wings. 'The pipistrelle bats are back. I thought the
builders had disturbed them when they mended the
chimney.' If she kept prattling, maybe he would tell
her where he was going.

'I'm just on my way out. Have you had supper?'

'No,' she lied. Whatever he was having, she would
force it down.

'How about the Coach and Horses? They do an
excellent steak.'

She swallowed. 'I'm off steak, but a salad would be
nice. Something light. . .I don't eat much in the
evenings.'

'Your hair's growing again,' he said, taking his eyes
off the moonlit road for an instant.

She put her hand to her head, feeling the soft stubble
that was beginning to curl up again. 'Mmm, I'll
have to go back to that swanky salon that Jennifer
uses.'

'Don't.'

She felt his hand over hers and stiffened, at first
with apprehension and then with anticipation. It was

the first time he'd touched her for over two weeks. Almost immediately he removed his hand.

'Why not?'

'Because I think I prefer the burning bush. It's more. . .you. Besides, you don't want to look like all the run-of-the-mill dolly birds. . .'

'I am not a dolly bird!'

'Exactly! You're a unique person, Lauren, a one-off, so stop trying to change yourself.'

'But I thought you wanted me to change. . .' Her voice trailed away as she realised what she'd said.

'And does my opinion matter to you?' His voice was husky.

'Whatever gave you that idea?' she said, quickly.

They were pulling into the car park. There were spaces at the front of the pub but Russ deliberately drove round the back, parking the car as far away from the building as he could. He switched off the engine, turned towards Lauren and put out his hands.

'Shall we have a truce?' He was holding out both hands towards her.

She hesitated, but only for a moment before she went willingly into his arms, all the pent-up frustration burning up inside her. His lips were on her forehead. She moved her head so that he kissed her cheek, then her mouth. For how long they stayed with their lips together she had no idea. Suddenly, she realised that the gear shift on the automatic column between them was digging into her. She'd barely noticed it in the joy of being with Russ again.

Ruefully, she pulled away and leaned back against her seat.

'Hardly the most comfortable way to mend our quarrel,' Russ observed, with a wry grin.

She opened her eyes wide and fixed them on his face. 'Did we quarrel?'

'Let's say we had a temporary cold war. You took exception to what I said on the phone when all I wanted to do was share an omelette with you. I merely pointed out that. . .'

'Don't say it!' She put her fingers over his lips. 'I know what you said. . .and I'm working on it. . . but don't remind me. I don't want to spoil the evening again.'

He smiled down at her. 'Come on, let's go and eat. I'm starving.'

Lauren wished she could say the same! She made a tolerable attempt at eating her salad while she watched Russ tucking into a medium rare fillet steak.

'I like this place.' Russ looked across the table. 'I often have supper here.'

Lauren looked around the high oak-beamed ceiling. The dining area was perched on two levels above the bar lounge. The staircase was well worn and looked authentically old but she knew that the whole building was a modern reconstruction made from several cannibalised barns.

'I wondered where you went to in the evenings.'

He smiled. 'Ah, so you noticed!'

Oh, God, she loved that expression in his eyes! It was like chocolate creams, candy floss; it gave her the shivers all down her spine.

'I've got to ask you something—a professional matter.' She cleared her throat nervously.

'I thought you might. Otherwise you wouldn't be forcing your second supper down.'

She put her fork down on the plate and gave up the pretence. 'Have you booked your holiday yet?'

'What holiday?'

'Russell Harvey, you know perfectly well what I mean. In two weeks' time your contract finishes. You then have three months' leave before you go back to wherever it is you're going and. . .'

'Oh, that holiday! Three months lazing about in the Caribbean—I can't wait! All those dusky maidens in grass skirts. . .'

He was watching her face, judging just how long to go on teasing her. 'No, of course I haven't booked a holiday. In fact if you hadn't taken on another locum, I might have suggested I. . .'

'Oh, but I haven't got anyone. . .not yet. . .I mean I've had a lot of enquiries but there's no one experienced enough.'

She waited, hoping he would say something. She didn't want to beg. Oh, he wasn't making it easy for her!

'So, if you've got nothing planned,' she went on, after seconds had elapsed, 'maybe we could extend your contract.'

'Don't do me any favours,' he replied, breezily.

'I won't. I just. . .I just need you, that's all.' Her voice wavered. It was like a confessional, admitting that she wasn't a complete, independent person any more. 'In a professional way, that is,' she qualified, quickly.

He reached across and touched her cheek, his eyes shining with tenderness. 'Of course. Come on, I'll get the bill and then we'll go back for a nightcap.'

His fingers touched hers as they walked down the wooden staircase. She wasn't even aware of the other people around her as he held on to her hand.

Suddenly, she noticed one of her patients from the

well-woman clinic standing at the foot of the stairs, smiling up at the two doctors as they descended, hand in hand, totally wrapped up in each other.

'Hello, Dr Lauren. Enjoying a night out?'

Lauren put on her professional smile. 'Makes a change. Nice to see you again.' *Wish I could remember her name. She's a new patient. . .only seen her once since she moved into that house on the new estate.*

'I bet it'll be all round Oakwood by the end of the week,' she said to Russ as they drove out of the car park.

'Do you mind?' he asked, sharply.

She hesitated. 'I've got my reputation to think about.'

'You know, I was beginning to think you'd mellowed since I first met you, but underneath you haven't changed at all. You're still——'

'Don't say it, Russ!' she broke in, heatedly. 'I don't want to start up that argument again. We're having a truce tonight, remember?'

Closing her eyes, she leaned back against the soft seat, smelling the faint tang of the supple leather. She was mad with herself for breaking up the rapport that had been building up between them. Because she wanted tonight to be special. There was so little time before Russ would be going away.

They pulled into the courtyard. She went up the stairs ahead of him, her breathing accelerated by the feelings of excitement tinged with apprehension. He closed the door behind them. She leaned against him, feeling the beating of his heart through the thin cotton shirt, pounding against her breasts. Slowly, he brought his mouth down on to hers.

From the depths of their prolonged kiss she registered nothing but a desire to remain in his arms.

But, abruptly, he pulled away and went into the kitchen. She could hear him moving around, plugging in the kettle, putting cups on a tray.

He put a cup of tea on the small table beside her. She realised that tea was the last thing she wanted, but what would Russ think of her if she confessed her true feelings? She had no way of knowing how to deal with the situation. The last time she'd been in a man's apartment late at night, all those years ago, it had been awful, but she knew that Russ wouldn't be like that. He would be tender and patient with her. And she would be able to give in to all these sensual feelings he roused in her.

She watched him cautiously over the rim of the china cup. . . Aunt Maud had insisted on sending up a whole set of teacups so that the young doctor could enjoy his cuppa. Mugs were so uncivilised, according to Maud.

Suddenly he put down his cup. 'I'll walk you back to the house.'

She stood up, feeling nothing but frustration sweeping over her. 'It's been a lovely evening. And I'm glad you're staying on.'

'You sound as if you're proposing a vote of thanks at the Women's Institute.'

She bridled. 'Do I?'

'Only joking, Lauren.'

He touched her cheek and gently kissed her on the lips.

It was a brief kiss. She stood stock still, savouring the sensuous feeling that rippled between them.

'So, I can tell Dad that you're staying on till the end of your leave?' she said, breezily. 'And then what will you do? Where's your next port of call?'

'Now you're fishing. The options are endless, but it's not easy to make a decision. . .at the moment.'

'No, of course not.' She started to move towards the door.

They walked across the courtyard, round the side of the surgery, across the gravel drive and up the stone steps. He waited as she fished out her key.

'Goodnight, Lauren.'

He bent to drop a kiss on her cheek but she turned her head so that their lips met.

And then, very quickly, she ran inside, enjoying the look of surprise on his face.

CHAPTER ELEVEN

'WHY did this have to happen on the last day of the school holidays?'

Lauren looked sympathetically at the distraught mother, cradling her sobbing six-year-old son.

'He's only had that bike two days. I told his dad to leave the stabilisers on, but oh, no, he has to prove how clever he is. David can balance; he's a big boy now. . .'

'Yes, it's bad luck.' Lauren leaned forward from her deskside chair in her consulting-room. There was a waiting-room full of patients but Ruth had brought young David Robinson in as soon as the worried mother and son arrived. 'I'm just going to take a peep at your hand, David.'

More loud wails as David tried to hide the injured hand. Mrs Robinson had loosely bound it in a crêpe bandage after he'd fallen off the bike and Lauren could see the swelling around the fingers. She wished the mother had left it untouched and brought David straight to the surgery.

'Would you like a ride on my stretcher?'

There was a flicker of interest in the small patient's eyes and the sobbing eased off.

'Where to?' David asked warily.

'Oh, just across the corridor. You know that nice room with the rocking horse where——'

'You're not going to prick me with a needle?'

'Definitely not, I promise.' Lauren remembered that

it was only a few weeks since David had been in the treatment-room for some booster jabs. Because he'd wriggled, Sister Fiona had unavoidably spoiled her record of painless injections.

She fiddled with the intercom and got through to the treatment-room. 'Sister, could you bring the stretcher through—have you anyone with you? Well, finish off your ECG and then come on through.

'While we're waiting for your ride I'll just take a peep. . .there now, that didn't hurt, did it?'

Having removed the makeshift bandage, Lauren was able to make an initial diagnosis. The pain was obvious and there was weakness, loss of movement, swelling and tenderness in the anatomical snuffbox area of the wrist, over the scaphoid. In her experience she'd found that the scaphoid bone was the commonest site of fracture in the carpus. That's what it probably was, but she'd check it out on her new X-ray machine.

She looked down at the little boy, still cuddled against his mother. She could, of course, get the ambulance and have him shipped to hospital. But the journey would be uncomfortable and frightening for him; he'd have to sit around in Casualty getting more and more upset. She knew she was a softie where her little patients were concerned but she hated to see them suffer unnecessarily. That was one reason she'd insisted on getting the X-ray machine. She could confirm her own clinical diagnoses and commence treatment. Sister Fiona had been sent off on an orthopaedic course to learn how to apply plaster of Paris. Russ had said that very soon there wouldn't be much she couldn't do here, short of open-heart surgery.

The thought made her smile inside as she remembered his words. He'd certainly helped her to improve the medical facilities here in the five months he'd been with her. Was it really five months? She felt the now familiar twinge of anxiety when she thought of how the time was flying. Only a month to go and nothing resolved yet.

She wondered, fleetingly, where Russ had gone off to today, so mysteriously. He'd insisted on a morning off and given her no reason for it. She'd seen him driving off soon after breakfast.

He's probably got an appointment with someone from the World Health Organisation about his next assignment, she thought. That would be why he'd insisted she shake up the staffing arrangements here at the surgery. He'd advised her to take on two more full-time doctors; he'd even helped her draft out the job specifications, so that she couldn't procrastinate any longer. . .

'You wanted the special transport wagon, Doctor.' Sister Fiona Grey stood in the doorway, smiling across the room, one hand steadying the stretcher. 'Now, David, what have you been up to?'

'Another summer holiday casualty, I'm afraid,' Lauren said, as she eased the little boy from his mother's arms and laid him on the stretcher.

'It's been a busy summer,' Sister Fiona said. 'I'll be glad to get my own children back in school next week.'

They certainly had been inundated with accidents during the long school holidays. Cuts, bruises, fractures, burns. . .as Lauren thought briefly over the last couple of months she realised she'd hardly had time to catch her breath. Certainly had no time to brood or worry. . .which was a good thing.

The pale September sun was shining in through the slatted louvre windows in the treatment-room. Lauren adjusted the blinds to obscure the light. Carefully she lifted David on to the X-ray table, feeling once again the surge of pride that she'd actually managed to persuade the accountants that she could balance the books with this one. Since taking Russ's advice and opting to run the surgery as an independent trust she'd made so many vital changes. She would never have dared to contemplate them on her own. It was good of him to take such an interest in the place. . .especially when he would be moving on soon. . .

She banished the unpleasant thought to concentrate on her little patient. Taking her time, so as not to upset him again, she carefully radiographed the injured wrist from four different angles so as to be sure of her diagnosis.

Sure enough, when she checked the X-rays, the unmistakable fracture in the scaphoid could be seen. She knew that manipulation wouldn't be required because the displacement would be corrected by immobilising the wrist in slight extension.

Her small patient cheered up considerably when the scaphoid plaster was complete. Lauren had helped Sister Fiona to include the thumb as far as the interphalangeal joint to allow opposition to the index finger. It left the little patient's left hand in a slightly raised position but Lauren knew that he wouldn't find it uncomfortable when he got used to it.

'How long will it have to stay on, Doctor?' Mrs Robinson asked in an apprehensive tone.

'It varies according to how quickly the bone heals. I'll X-ray it again in four weeks. We usually say four to twelve weeks—but twelve weeks is unusually long. Something in between the two, I would say at this stage.'

The backlog of patients caused by the emergency took her well into her lunch break. Ian Fairburn came back from the morning house calls and found her just about to eat an apple at her desk.

'The blue-eyed boy not back yet?' he asked. 'Where's he gone?'

Lauren frowned. She hadn't invited Ian to walk straight in and she certainly objected to his over-familiarity. He must have realised by now that she was still annoyed at the way he'd behaved on the day the flu epidemic started but he'd made no attempt to apologise. Neither she nor Russ had mentioned the episode again so it was still unresolved. But on top of that Ian had voiced his objections to every new move she'd made in recent weeks. He was an old stick-in-the-mud and she'd be better off without him!

'I've no idea where he's gone. I pride myself in minding my own business, which is more than I can say for. . .'

'Oh, hoity toity, are we? Look here, Lauren. I'm beginning to get a bit tired of being your dogsbody. I don't like the way you're making all these changes. I preferred the surgery how it was when your father ran it and. . .'

'Well, you're quite free to leave if that's what you're hinting at!'

For an instant, neither of them spoke. Ian Fairburn's eyes showed how stunned he was.

'That wasn't what I was hinting at at all, but if you want me to leave. . .'

She glared back. 'I want you to think carefully about your future.' Ye gods, she was sounding just like her old headmistress that time she'd been caught swimming in the pool when she should have been doing her prep!

But once she'd got the bit between her teeth there was no stopping her. 'I'm going to continue making changes here until I've got the place as efficient and streamlined as I possibly can. I'm going to take on extra staff, expand the well-woman clinic. . .'

She paused for breath, hoping he would say something but he remained silent. It was as if he couldn't take it all in.

'Listen, Ian, we've been friends a long time.' She changed the headmistress tone. 'But nothing ever stands still. If you're not happy here any more, you'd better think about moving on somewhere.'

'I'll leave at the end of the month. You'd better get a replacement for October.' His voice was dry, expressionless, like a patient suffering from shock.

Now she was the one who couldn't think of anything to say. Events were moving too quickly. Russ was leaving at the end of the month. If Ian left. . .

'If that's what you want,' she heard herself say, once more the headmistress.

A squeal of brakes could be heard in the courtyard.

'That will be Russ,' Ian Fairburn said, his tone bitter. 'He's got a lot to answer for, has that man, coming here and turning everything upside-down. We could have been happy together, Lauren, you and I.'

She stared at him. The vague suspicions that had been forming in her mind were now confirmed. He was desperately jealous of Russ, not just of his forthright go-ahead medical ideas but of his supposed claim on her affections.

'It's just as well things have come to a head,' she said, carefully. 'Because I could never have contemplated anything other than a platonic friendship with you, Ian. I'm sure I never led you to believe otherwise.

We've had some good times here at the surgery. You've been a good doctor. . .correction, you *are* a good doctor. So wherever you move on to I'll give you a good reference.'

It was all so final; she was giving the end-of-term speech up on the rostrum now, cap and gown firmly in place. She stood up as if to emphasise that the interview was over. The door opened and Russ walked in.

'Oh, am I disturbing something? Perhaps I should have knocked. Hang on, I'll go out and come in again.'

'Oh, don't be so stupid!' Lauren snapped.

'I'm just going,' Ian Fairburn said, moving swiftly out through the door. 'Lauren will fill you in on the details.'

'What was all that about?' Russ perched on the edge of Lauren's desk, his expressive eyes scanning her face.

'I'll tell you all about it later,' Lauren said, wearily. 'Ian's given in his notice.'

'How very sad!' Russ said, his face wreathed in smiles.

'I think I'll be running this place single-handed from October.'

'No, you won't. You've been grossly understaffed for years. The budget will stretch to more staff and I'll help you appoint them. You need more time for yourself Lauren, more time to be a woman.'

'Ah, we're back to my womanly qualities again, are we?' She tossed the half-eaten apple into the waste bin and looked up into the perceptive blue eyes.

'Did you miss me?' he asked, a whimsical smile on his face.

'Only because I was rushed off my feet all morning and could have done with some help,' she replied, ungraciously. 'Incidentally, where did you go?'

'Ask no questions and I'll tell you no lies.'

'Why all the mystery?'

'Come out with me this evening and I'll reveal all.'

'Promises, promises!'

'Straight after surgery. We'll have a drink in the flat first. . .and before you say that Aunt Maud wants you to hold the wool for her knitting. . .'

'I wasn't going to say anything.'

She saw the surprise in his eyes.

'So you'll come out with me this evening?' he asked, in a diffident tone.

She smiled. 'Might as well. Mind you, I'll have to cancel all my other engagements, so I hope it will be worth it.'

Lauren came out of her consulting-room as soon as the last patient had departed that evening. She'd made the effort to change between the afternoon clinic and this evening. She smoothed her hands over the linen skirt, turned back the cuffs on her silk blouse. She felt very feminine. She'd even showered and changed her underwear in her tea break, Aunt Maud knocking on the bathroom door and asking if she was feeling all right. Dear Aunt Maud; she couldn't understand any change in routine. Baths were taken in the morning and the evening but never at teatime.

'You're looking charming,' Russ said as he came down the stairs.

'Well, thank you, kind sir. . . Oh, goodnight, Ruth,' Lauren called as her worthy helpmeet left her station.

'Going somewhere nice, you two?' Ruth asked.

'We haven't decided yet,' Russ said, quickly. 'We've got some unfinished business to discuss first.'

'Ohhh. . .?' Ruth stood by the outer door, waiting in hope that someone would enlighten her, but no one did.

Lauren locked the outer door of the surgery behind them, checking that the security lights were working. She was feeling decidedly nervous. There was some sort of showdown in the offing. She could feel it in her bones.

'Coffee?' he asked, as soon as Lauren was settled on the window seat.

'Have you anything stronger?'

He blinked. This wasn't the cautious girl he knew!

'I could crack open a bottle of wine, but if I join you in a glass I won't be able to drive and we'll have to stay in.'

'So?'

She was staring at him with that forthright 'what's the problem?' expression. He went to the kitchen in search of the corkscrew. 'Red or white?'

'I don't mind.'

'I've got a really good bottle of claret I've been saving for a special occasion. I'll open that.'

'So, it's a special occasion, is it?' Lauren asked, feeling a decided increase in her pulse-rate.

'Could be,' he replied in an enigmatic voice.

He handed her a glass and for a few seconds they sipped in silence.

'I went to see Peter Hardcastle this morning,' he announced, quietly.

Lauren spluttered and put down her wine. 'You what?'

'I went to see your ex-boyfriend,' he replied in a dead pan voice.

'He was not my boyfriend!' Lauren said, fiercely.

'We went out together three times and the third time he. . .'

'Yes, go on,' Russ said, gently.

She took a deep breath. 'He tried to rape me.'

All of a sudden the familiar room seemed very quiet.

'That's what I thought,' Russ said, in an ominous tone. 'He tried to deny it but I knew he was lying.'

'But why did you go to see him? What made you ask him about it?' She realised she was trembling as the awful memories flooded back.

'Because I wanted to know why you'd turned your back on normal feelings of love and sensuality. Oh, I knew your background was partly to blame. . .no, hear me out!' he insisted as she tried to remonstrate.

'Being the doctor's daughter, the mainstay of the practice, all that didn't help, but I sensed there was something more. When we first met you told me you planned to remain single. You were so adamant about it, so absolutely sure that you didn't want to be part of a physical relationship. I became convinced that something, or somebody, must have turned off your sensual emotions. Then when I saw your reaction to Peter Hardcastle in hospital I decided that he must have upset you in some way and that he might be the one responsible for making you frigid.'

'I am not frigid!' Lauren protested.

'But you were,' he said. 'When I first met you. I was frightened of laying a finger on you.'

'But I've changed!' She realised she was almost screaming and she didn't care who heard her any more.

'I think you have,' he said, slowly. 'But I wanted to know the full story before I asked you.'

'Asked me what?' she flung at him impatiently. 'And why did you have to go and see Peter Hardcastle?

Didn't he think it strange, my locum asking him all those personal questions?'

'He did, as a matter of fact. But when I told him I was going to ask you to marry me he understood.'

'You told him what?' She could feel the room spinning around her. She closed her eyes, then opened them again to make sure she wasn't dreaming. Nothing was real any more. Had Russ said he wanted to marry her?

'I told him I wanted to marry you,' Russ repeated, gently. 'Because that's exactly what I want to do. And don't look at me as if I've taken leave of my senses. I want us to be together and I know that the only way we can make that happen is by getting married. With your background, Lauren, you're not going to agree to an affair. . .'

'Always harping on about my background. Let me be the judge of whether I want an affair or not!'

'Well, would you?' he asked, quietly.

She hesitated. 'I don't know,' she said, slowly. Russ knew her so well! It would be so difficult to shake off her conditioning. He was right. Her background had shaped the way she behaved but her decision not to marry had only come after her awful encounter with Peter. She'd felt she never wanted a man to touch her again, let alone spend the rest of her life with one. But Russ was different.

'It may surprise you to know that I've wanted you to make love to me every time we kissed,' she said, slowly. 'You've no idea how frustrated I've been when you simply walked away after we'd said goodnight.'

'And I was being oh, so careful not to frighten you. I wanted to find out the real reason why you were so frigid when I first met you. After a while I sensed a change in you but I had to hold back until I'd confirmed my suspicions.'

He drew her gently into his arms, nuzzling his mouth against her hair. 'I wouldn't hurt you, Lauren. I know that Peter put you off sexual relationships but now that I know the truth. . .'

'Make love to me now, Russ.'

Her voice betrayed the deep urgency she was feeling. For twelve years she'd ignored the sexual side of herself but here in Russ's arms she felt alive again. And she knew she could trust him completely. It was as if, in discovering the awful truth about Peter, Russ had exorcised the entire unsavoury episode. Any fears she'd had were completely gone. Now, as she looked up into his eyes she saw surprise mingled with tenderness.

'Are you sure that's what you want, Lauren?' he asked, gently.

'I'm sure,' she whispered.

He stood up, holding out a hand to pull her against him. Her feet felt incredibly light as she moved into the bedroom, shedding her clothes as she walked, stepping over the new lacy undies that she was now so glad she'd invested in.

The cotton sheet felt deliciously cool against her cheek as she lay waiting. He climbed in beside her and as their skins touched she let out an involuntary moan. He held her close for a few seconds, not moving.

'You're quite safe, Lauren,' he murmured gently.

'I know,' she whispered. This was where she belonged.

She felt a tremor of excitement running down Russ's body and it transmitted itself to her. She could feel the raw pent-up passion building up inside her; she was holding herself back, still unsure if she could go along with the new sensations.

'Oh, yes,' she murmured against his mouth as she eased herself against his caressing fingers. Her body was made of liquid fire; nothing could douse the flames now. He was so tender and gentle with her. She'd never imagined it would be like this in all those years when she'd spurned all physical contact. He was driving her to fever pitch with his caresses and all the time she wanted more. . .she wanted the ultimate fulfilment. . .

As he entered her she cried out with the sheer joy of knowing that she was at one with him. And then their passion fused with the ecstatic union until wave after orgasmic wave sent her into unbelievable ecstasy. . .

It was Russ's arm under her shoulder that woke her. She wasn't used to having another person beside her in bed. Outside, a quarter moon was shining on the top of the garage.

What was she doing here in Russ's flat and why did she feel so elated? And then as the memories of their lovemaking flooded back she gave a deep sigh of contentment. So that was what it was really like! And to think she'd been denying herself all these years. But she was sure that only Russ could have made it so special.

She raised her head and looked down at the sleeping figure.

He stirred in his sleep as she moved to get out of bed, suddenly remembering the reality of the situation. It was two o'clock in the morning. How was she going to explain this?

'Don't go!' He was reaching for her, pulling her back amid the rumpled sheets.

She turned and smiled down at him ruefully. 'I ought to make a move if I'm going to salvage my honour.'

'Bit late for that, I would have thought,' he murmured, sleepily, pulling her against him. 'The only way you can do that is to marry me. I'm still waiting for your answer.'

She stared up into the tender blue eyes. 'But what about your job. . .my job. . .all the problems of living together? And you don't want to settle down, and I can't leave here and. . .'

'Hush, stop worrying. It won't be easy but we'll find a way.'

'But it's all so sudden. I mean the idea takes some getting used to. You just spring this upon me and expect. . .'

'Stop worrying; we'll work something out. The main question is, do you want to marry me?'

She took a deep breath, her head spinning round with problems, real and imaginary. She couldn't take it all in. She loved this man so much, but marriage! How could they possibly combine their differing lifestyles, she with her general practice and Russ flying off all over the world?

'I'd like to think about it before I give you my answer.'

His eyes held a veiled, enigmatic expression as he looked down at her.

'Well, don't take too long. Time's running out.'

CHAPTER TWELVE

IN THE cold light of day, she knew that the idea of marriage to Russ was wonderful, but how could they make it work? How could they possibly combine their disparate lifestyles? One or both of them would have to give up their jobs and that would only lead to feelings of resentment against each other. Just supposing she were to ask Russ to stop travelling the world and settle down here at the practice with her. Maybe it would work for a while, but he'd soon get itchy feet and she wouldn't want him to feel she'd clipped his wings. She simply couldn't do that to him. She loved him too much!

As soon as he walked into the surgery she called him into her consulting-room.

'About last night. . .'

He pulled her against him, and nuzzled his face against her hair.

'No, wait, Russ, we have to be objective about this. It doesn't help if. . .'

She sighed as his lips closed over hers. Nothing would ever douse the flames of their love, but marriage was out of the question. She could see the future lying ahead of them as they forged their separate ways, meeting up occasionally for a few snatched days of ecstatic passion before one of them had to move on. . . until Russ found himself a girl with no responsibilities, who hadn't taken on the family firm, who didn't have so many people depending on her.

'We've got to talk,' she said, coming up for air. 'Sit there, Russell, and don't touch me till I've finished.'

'Yes, ma'am!'

He sat in the patients' chair alongside her. 'OK, don't tell me, you've had second thoughts. I can see it in your face.'

She glanced nervously at the clock. The first patients were arriving outside in the waiting-room. The relentless stream would start flowing and she wouldn't have a minute to herself.

'It wouldn't work. . .not marriage. Perhaps we could have an affair—meet each other now and then. . .'

'Is that what you want, Lauren, an affair?'

She swallowed the lump in her throat. 'No, of course it's not. I want the whole works like any other woman. A husband, children. . .'

She broke off, wondering who'd put those conventional words into her mouth. But it was true! Suddenly, she knew she'd been denying all her inner instincts for so long she hadn't recognised what was happening to her. And now this wretched, wonderful man had come along and disturbed all her carefully made plans for a secure, predictable, eminently professional life.

'And I want you to be my wife,' he said, slowly, leaning forward to take hold of her hands before moving quickly back, remembering that she didn't want to be confused by physical contact.

'Shall I send the first patient in, Dr Lauren?'

Lauren glared at the offending intercom. 'Give me two minutes, Ruth. I'm busy right now.'

'Take your time, Doctor,' Ruth replied, in her motherly 'I know what's best' voice. 'There's nothing urgent. Buzz me when you've finished your talk.'

Russ gave a wry grin. 'Ruth doesn't miss a trick, does she? She watched me coming in here this morning and wished me luck.'

'I wish she wouldn't interfere,' Lauren snapped.

'And I wish she would! It's high time someone tried to talk some sense into that thick skull of yours.'

'Well, thank you very much, Doctor, for this enlightening discussion. Now, if you don't mind I've got work to do.'

'Lauren, this won't get us anywhere. Last night. . .'

'Last night we were in cloud cuckoo land. This is the real world. At the end of the month you'll be jetting off to the tropics, leaving me to. . .'

'I don't have to. I could take a job closer to home. . .closer to you, Lauren.'

She swallowed. 'And would you be willing to do that, Russ?'

'Yes, I would.'

She scanned his face, searching for any sign of hesitation. He looked so sincere, but inside was he feeling the shades of the prison closing in? Would he, in years to come, accuse her of clipping his wings? She couldn't do that to the man she loved.

Slowly, she shook her head. 'I can't marry you, Russ.'

He stood up. 'You're an impossibly stubborn girl. I can't think what I see in you.'

She gave a rueful smile. 'Neither can I.'

He couldn't resist putting out a playful hand and mussing up her newly brushed hair.

'Get out before I throw you out!' she said, and then put out a restraining hand to hold on to him for just a few seconds longer. 'No hard feelings?'

'What do you think?'

She watched the closing door, the awful feeling of finality sweeping over her. She'd heard the bitterness in his tone. This was the end. They couldn't meet halfway any more. Russ had set the ultimatum. It was all or nothing.

For the next couple of weeks, Lauren threw herself into her work, deliberately blotting out the niggling doubts at the back of her mind. She was doing the right thing, the honourable thing, taking the sensible course of action as she always had done. Russ would disappear from her life and she would forget him. She would forget him. . .

Whenever she really contemplated a Russ-less future she felt sick to her stomach. But she told herself she would get over him. She'd been perfectly happy with her life before he'd come along and turned her world upside-down.

He seemed to be tying up the loose ends at the end of his contract, taking more and more time to go up to London for interviews and meetings. She didn't enquire; he would inform her when his next overseas assignment was finalised.

Meanwhile, she'd been busy interviewing prospective candidates for the practice. She'd taken Russ's advice and agreed to take on three more full-time doctors. He'd pointed out that with the influx of extra patients from the new housing estate the practice would have to expand, and the economics of his proposition was quite sound. There had been a good number of candidates to chose from, now that the positions were permanent.

She'd asked Russ to sit in on the interviews as she valued the help he gave her on these occasions.

'So, by the end of the month there'll be four of you full-time,' Russ had observed, as they drank coffee in her consulting-room at the end of one of the interviews. 'I liked the look of this young man. Good qualifications, dependable, excellent track record and references. You could do a lot worse, Lauren.'

'Four doctors in one practice. It seems a lot,' she said, remembering the old days when her father managed all by himself.

'The practice has expanded to fit the needs of the community and you've gone along with everything so far. Don't hold back. In fact I think you should retain a part-time doctor as well, someone you can call in on a temporary basis if the work piles up.'

'I've had enough interviewing for one month.' She leaned her head against the back of the chair.

'I'll find someone for you. . .before I go.'

'Thanks.' She looked out of the window at the late afternoon September sun, slanting over the garden. The end of the summer. . .the end of an era for her.

But it was a new beginning. Three new doctors to train, and the possibility of a part-timer. Ian Fairburn had found himself a hospital appointment in Chelmsford and was looking forward to his new job. Lauren was relieved that they were still on speaking terms and that none of the patients had commented on his unexpected imminent departure. He'd never been over-popular with the patients. Lauren secretly thought that he'd work better in the more rarefied atmosphere of a hospital.

'Oh, Aunt Maud wants you to come to supper before you go,' Lauren said, as casually as possible. She'd been putting off the invitation as long as she could, hoping that her aunt would forget about it. But no, she'd been reminded again this morning at breakfast.

'Such a pity we're going to lose that young man. Just when he was settling in nicely,' had been the poignant words that hadn't helped the start of Lauren's day one bit.

'I'm a bit tied up at the moment. Maybe one day next week.'

'Fine. Just let me know a day in advance so that Aunt Maud has time to prepare the last supper.'

'That's what it will be, won't it, Lauren?'

She nodded, not trusting herself to speak. That's right, she thought. Twist the knife in. She was functioning on automatic pilot and could do without these nasty reminders of the march of time.

Lauren glanced at the wall calendar in the kitchen. No one had pulled off yesterday's date. She ripped it off viciously, exposing the awesome fact that it was the last Wednesday in September. From the drawing-room she could hear the murmur of convivial voices. Russ was entertaining her father with stories of his exploits in Africa. Aunt Maud had insisted she join her in the kitchen to prepare the French dressing for the salad.

'I'm no good at the foreign touches. You're so much better than me at it, Lauren,' her aunt was saying as Lauren mixed the olive oil and wine vinegar together with a sprinkling of herbs.

Lauren glanced down at the elderly lady, surprised at the humble tone. Aunt Maud didn't usually confess that she was inferior to anyone in any situation. And Lauren knew for a fact that her aunt was famed for her French cookery, having taken a cordon bleu course in her youth. She was up to something! That was why she'd been spirited away from the men.

'I'm not one to interfere, Lauren. . .'

Not much!

'. . .but when I have something to say I say it. Look, would you mind putting down that spoon and closing the door? I don't want your father to hear me talking to you in here.'

Here we go. What have I done now? Lauren thought as she closed the kitchen door and moved over to one of the fireside chairs. Might as well make herself comfortable if she was going to get a lecture.

'You may think I've been hard on you sometimes, Lauren. All those times when I used to visit you when you were a child and later when I came to live here after your poor mother died. . .'

Lauren raised her eyes and watched apprehensively as her aunt sank down into the other fireside chair, carefully smoothing out her skirts so as to cover her knees.

'. . .but I believed it was for your own good. I pride myself that I was influencing you into becoming a strong, independent girl. . .'

'Look, Aunt Maud, has this got anything to do with our dinner tonight? Because if we don't get a move on that leg of lamb will be burned to a cinder. Can't this wait until——?'

'No, it can't wait! Because time and tide, my girl, wait for no man.'

'Yes, that's true,' Lauren conceded, stunned by the emotional tone.

'You may find this hard to believe, but when I was young I was quite attractive and I had a number of boyfriends—one in particular was. . .very special at the time.'

Lauren stared at her aunt. There was the hint of a

blush on the pale, wrinkled cheeks. It sounded as if she was in for one of those woman-to-woman sessions. She'd only ever had one of these from Aunt Maud. It was in her early teens. Her mother had just been diagnosed as having leukaemia and had gone into hospital for a few weeks. Aunt Maud had come over during the school holidays to help out and been asked by her brother to check that the girls understood about menstruation. Lauren remembered how she'd put her out of her misery by announcing that they'd done it in biology. But she was a bit old now for a further expansion on the facts of life. . .

'Well, anyway, he asked me to marry him. He was going away overseas and he wanted us to marry before he went. . .'

I don't believe it! Lauren thought as the penny dropped. The scheming. . .

'I told him I couldn't marry him because I wanted to have a career. It was a conscious decision I made at that time and I didn't regret it. I enjoyed my teaching career, my years as a headmistress were infinitely fulfilling, but, you know, as I get older, I sometimes wonder if I missed out. It's only human nature to want a husband and children. In my young days you had to choose between a career or marriage. It was either or. But times have changed; you, Lauren, could have both. . .'

Total silence except for the ticking of the clock on the mantelpiece. Lauren drew in her breath as she watched the unfamiliar spectacle of her aunt lost for words.

The older woman took out her handkerchief and blew her nose. 'You may wonder why I'm telling you this. Well, I'm not totally unaware of what's been going on and I have the feeling that you might be letting a wonderful opportunity slip through your fingers.'

'But you've always been so. . .so dead against marriage,' Lauren put in falteringly.

'I used to be. . .the old idea of marriage where a wife was nothing but a glorified skivvy. But exciting things have been happening over the years and young women can have careers and marriage, so what I'm saying is. . .'

The kitchen door opened and Russ stood on the threshold, looking quizzically from one to the other of them.

'I came to see if you ladies would join us for a drink. Is everything all right?'

Lauren jumped to her feet. 'Fine! My aunt was just reminiscing about old times.' She leaned across the fireplace and planted a kiss on the older woman's forehead. 'Come on, Aunt Maud. Go and have a sherry. I'll join you when I've rescued the sacrificial lamb.'

Lauren tried to keep the conversation round the supper table deliberately light. She changed the subject whenever talk of future plans began. She felt as if she were in a state of limbo, mulling over her aunt's words which had affected her more than she cared to admit.

When her father went upstairs to bed, Aunt Maud immediately followed, saying she was going to have an early night. When Russ offered to help her father Lauren saw how pleased the older man was.

She stayed on at the table, going over and over how she could resolve the marriage problem for herself and Russ but there seemed no answer. It was all very well for Aunt Maud to talk about marriage and a career but the practicalities of the situation in her own case were impossible!

She got up from the table and went into the kitchen, busying herself with the clearing up.

'I'll help you with the dishes.' Russ came up behind her.

'No, that's OK. I've nearly finished stacking the dishwasher. Mrs Parsons will empty it in the morning. She's having a half-day to go and visit her sister in hospital.'

Lauren straightened up as she slammed shut the door of the machine, pressing the button and turning around.

He was standing oh, so close. . .too close for comfort.

'Is my father settled?' she asked, quietly. Russ had taken the older man up to his room and shared the obligatory nightcap.

'I was afraid you might have gone to bed already.'

'I'll go soon. Got a busy day tomorrow.'

'Your aunt went to bed early tonight.'

'Yes, didn't she?' Clearing the decks, leaving me alone with my decision. Maud's words were still ringing in her ears.

'Look, Russ. . .'

'Look, Lauren. . .'

They laughed as they broke the awkward silence simultaneously.

He walked across to the fireplace and tossed another log into the grate. Sparks fragmented over the iron fender. He turned to face her.

'I've got a suitable candidate for that part-time post,' he told her in a matter-of-fact tone.

'Any good?' she asked, without enthusiasm.

'That's for you to decide.'

'Where did you find this one?'

'Very close to home, actually. He works for the World Health Organisation.'

Her legs felt weak. She sat down on one of the wooden chairs by the kitchen table.

'Is this someone I know?'

He crossed the room and put his hands on her shoulders.

'Hear me out, Lauren, before you turn down my plan.'

He moved around the table and sat down facing her, his hands clasped in front of him.

'I've engineered myself a part-time lecturing post, seconded from the World Health Organisation and based in London at the School of Tropical Medicine. This means I would be free to take on other medical work on a part-time basis. Some of my lecturing would require travel within the United Kingdom; occasionally I would have to travel overseas, but I would only agree to short periods abroad and I would insist on taking my wife. . .'

'Your wife?' Lauren repeated. 'But what if your wife was tied up with her own career. . .if she had staffing problems at her busy medical practice?'

'My wife wouldn't have staffing problems; I would see to that. My wife deserves some time to herself occasionally, some time to get to know her husband, maybe have a couple of children, simply live a little.'

'So you've got this part-time post based in London?'

He nodded. 'But I haven't got the part-time post at the medical practice. I've heard the senior partner is an absolute tartar. To be honest, I'm scared of applying.'

'I don't blame you. Would it help if I put in a word for you?'

'Oh, Lauren, would you?'

He was laughing as he came round the table and scooped her up into his arms.

Lauren didn't know whether she wanted to laugh or cry. It wasn't going to be easy combining their careers but they would work it out together. If Russ was happy to compromise, so was she.

His arms tightened about her as his kiss deepened.

'Put me down, Russ, before you give yourself a back injury,' she whispered against his lips as they paused for breath.

He lowered her gently to the ground, his arms still encircling her waist. 'Ever the practical one. I was about to carry you off to my den.'

'I thought you'd never ask. . .but save your strength for later and let me walk.'

He stared at her. 'How will you explain walking out in the middle of the night?'

'Easy; I'll leave a note.' And, grabbing hold of the kitchen scribble pad, she wrote in large letters so that everyone would read it, 'Gone to spend the night with Russ. Have plugged the calls through to his flat. Love, Lauren.'

He was smiling down at her, shaking his head in bewildered admiration. 'I've got to hand it to you, Lauren, I never thought the day would come when. . .'

'Come on, we're wasting time.'

'I'd love to see Aunt Maud's face when she reads that,' Russ said, as they escaped through the kitchen door.

Lauren glanced up at the dim bedroom light shining through a chink in the curtains. A small, frail figure enshrouded in a large nightgown was clutching at the curtains as she peered out. From the glimpse Lauren had she was sure her aunt's face was wreathed in smiles.

'So would I,' Lauren said, as she snuggled up against Russ.

EPILOGUE

THEY were married in the spring, at the little church in the village. It seemed as if the whole of Oakwood had turned out in full force to wish them luck.

The three new doctors were shaping up exceptionally well and Lauren had no qualms about leaving the surgery for a couple of weeks so that she and Russ could have a proper honeymoon. Her father had insisted that he be called in on an advisory capacity while Lauren and Russ were away, if there was anything the young doctors couldn't handle. Lauren had told them that her father would be overjoyed to keep his hand in, so if a situation where he was required could be engineered it would help to keep the reluctant convalescent from getting bored.

On their return from honeymoon they were going to live in the flat until their new house was ready. Maud and James Mansfield had wanted the newly-weds to move in with them but Russ and Lauren had been adamant about keeping their independence. They'd bought a plot of land just down the lane and the builders were making a start even at that very moment.

Lauren firmly clenched the pen as she signed the register in the vestry of the church. From through the door, she could hear the choir singing 'Jesu, Joy of Man's Desiring'.

The service had gone so quickly. Was she really married to this man, as the vicar had just pronounced?

She caught her breath as the sleeve of Russ's jacket brushed across her satin bodice. Who would ever have thought that she would have allowed herself to be decked out like this? She glanced in the huge mirror over the vestry fireplace and barely recognised the conventional-looking bride who smiled back at her. Thank goodness the head-dress concealed most of her hair. It had taken a multitude of hairpins and clips to secure it. The minute she took it off her hair would spring out around her again.

She caught her breath at the thought of taking off her head-dress, at being able to escape all the razzmatazz of the reception to be alone with Russ. She had no idea where he was taking her on honeymoon and she didn't care. He'd said it was somewhere hot, so pack a bikini or two. But who cared about clothes... or the lack of them? They were escaping for two whole weeks together, without a care in the world. . .

'You're looking very lovely, Mrs Harvey,' Russ whispered, so quietly that no one else in the mêlée around them heard.

'My name is Dr Lauren Mansfield,' she whispered back. 'I'm not going to change my working name for you or anybody.'

'I'm not talking about your working title. It's your off-duty title that interests me. Just so long as you remember you're my wife tonight. . .'

'When you two have finished whispering we'll be able to go back down the aisle,' Aunt Maud said, coming up behind them and whisking her hand over the crumpled lace of Lauren's head-dress. 'Really, Lauren, you'll have to do something about your hair. . . Now stand still!' This last rejoinder to Lauren's young nieces who were dancing around excitedly in their pale pink crinolines, tripping over the unaccustomed length of their skirts.

Lauren braced herself as she heard the organist starting up the Mendelssohn Wedding March. The vestry door was opening; necks were craning to get a glimpse of them. She could see her sisters in their new designer suits standing on tiptoe so as not to miss anything. And there was Caroline, Russ's sister, who'd come over from America with her new husband especially for the wedding. Russ had been so happy when his sister announced that she was getting married to the orthopaedic consultant who'd taken care of her since her accident. Another fairy-tale ending!

Behind them a blur of familiar faces, all smiling, everyone looking so happy. Ruth with her husband and children, looking incredibly smart. . .

'Once more unto the breach,' she whispered to Russ, holding tightly on to his arm to stop her knees from trembling. 'I don't know why we agreed to go through with all this. If only my father had propped a ladder up against my bedroom window. . .'

'Yes, why didn't he? We could have been halfway to Timbuctoo by now.'

'Is that where we're going?'

'Wouldn't you like to know. . .?'

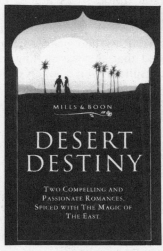
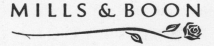

HEARTS OF FIRE

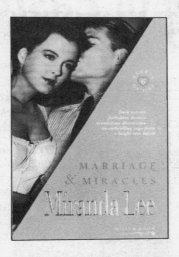

Gemma's marriage to Nathan is in tatters, but she is sure she can win him back if only she can teach him the difference between lust and love…

She knows she's asking for a miracle, but miracles can happen, can't they?

The answer is in Book 6…

MARRIAGE & MIRACLES
by Miranda Lee

The final novel in the compelling HEARTS OF FIRE saga.

Available from August 1994   Priced: £2.50

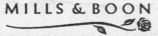

MILLS & BOON

SUMMER SPECIAL!

Four exciting new Romances for the price of three

Each Romance features British heroines and their encounters with dark and desirable Mediterranean men. *Plus, a free Elmlea recipe booklet inside every pack.*

So sit back and enjoy your sumptuous summer reading pack and indulge yourself with the free Elmlea recipe ideas.

Available July 1994   Price £5.70

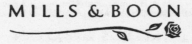

MILLS & BOON

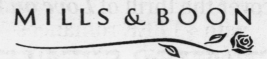

MILLS & BOON

LOVE ON CALL

The books for enjoyment this month are:

HEARTS OUT OF TIME Judith Ansell
THE DOCTOR'S DAUGHTER Margaret Barker
MIDNIGHT SUN Rebecca Lang
ONE CARING HEART Marion Lennox

♥   ♥   ♥   ♥   ♥

Treats in store!

Watch next month for the following absorbing stories:

ROLE PLAY Caroline Anderson
CONFLICTING LOYALTIES Lilian Darcy
ONGOING CARE Mary Hawkins
A DEDICATED VET Carol Wood

Discover the thrill of *Love on Call* with 4 FREE romances

FREE
BOOKS FOR YOU

In the exciting world of modern medicine, the emotions of true love acquire an added poignancy. Now you can experience these gripping stories of passion and pain, heartbreak and happiness - with Mills & Boon absolutely FREE! AND look forward to a regular supply of *Love on Call* delivered direct to your door.

🍎 🍎 🍎

Turn the page for details of how to claim 4 FREE books AND 2 FREE gifts!

An irresistible offer from Mills & Boon

Here's a very special offer from Mills & Boon for you to become a regular reader of *Love on Call*. And we'd like to welcome you with 4 books, a cuddly teddy bear and a special mystery gift - absolutely FREE and without obligation!

Then, every month look forward to receiving 4 brand new *Love on Call* romances delivered direct to your door for only £1.80 each. Postage and packing is FREE!

Plus a FREE Newsletter featuring authors, competitions, special offers and lots more...

This invitation comes with no strings attached. You may cancel or suspend your subscription at any time and still keep your FREE books and gifts.

It's so easy. Send no money now but simply complete the coupon below and return it today to:

Mills & Boon Reader Service, FREEPOST, PO Box 236, Croydon, Surrey CR9 9EL.

- - - - - - - NO STAMP NEEDED - - - - ✂

YES! Please rush me 4 FREE *Love on Call* romances and 2 FREE gifts! Please also reserve me a Reader Service subscription. If I decide to subscribe, I can look forward to receiving 4 brand new *Love on Call* romances for only £7.20 every month - postage and packing FREE. If I choose not to subscribe, I shall write to you within 10 days and still keep the FREE books and gifts. I may cancel or suspend my subscription at any time simply by writing to you. I am over 18 years of age.   Please write in BLOCK CAPITALS

Ms/Mrs/Miss/Mr _____ EP62D

Address _____

_____

_____ Postcode _____

Signature _____